Friends

of the

Deceased

A Trials of Katrina Novel

Dale J. Moore

Published by Northern Amusements, Inc., LaSalle, Ontario.

This is a work of fiction. All of the characters, organizations, and events portrayed in this novel are either products of the author's imagination or are used fictitiously.

Friends of the Deceased / Dale J. Moore - 1st Edition Trade Paperback

ISBN 978-0-98128173-5

This book and others by Northern Amusements are available in electronic format. Visit our web site at www.northernamusements.com.

e-Pub version
ISBN 978-0-98128174-2

e-PDF version
ISBN 978-0-98128175-9

Cover by Ami Moore

Author photo by Linda Moore

Printed and bound in the United States.

__Dedications__

To my wife Linda, who supports and encourages all my endeavours.

To my sister Maureen, whose story, characters, and talent inspired this book.

Dale J. Moore

0 *Salon*

Katrina stood in her salon, cutting the hair of one of her regular customers, Duncan. His twitching and restlessness was far worse than normal. She looked up from the nape of his neck and caught an image in the mirror in front of her. It was the reflection of a man outside the salon. The man held some bright orange papers in one hand, a stark contrast to the grey weather outside. One of the bright pages was held up with one hand by the man, before becoming firmly taped onto the window behind and to the right of Katrina. He continued to tape signs on each of the large windows of the store front, hesitating only slightly as he pinned up the one directly behind her. The writing on the pages faced outside.

   Katrina kept trimming Duncan's hair as she fixated on the man outside. She looked back to her customer and let out a short shrill at the blood on the back of his neck. Her loss of focus and Duncan's severe shaking had caused her to nick his skin. She applied pressure to the small cut, but it gushed around her finger. The bright orange blood streamed down Duncan's chest, causing him to scream and jump in his chair. Katrina held the dripping scissors and turned toward the front door. A pool of orange liquid formed around her feet. The stranger outside was attaching an orange leaflet onto the front door of Kat's Kuts. Katrina walked toward the door. Each step felt like a separate moment in time. As she neared the entrance, the door opened and the man stepped inside. The door slowly closed behind him, and she could see the writing on the papers – EVICTION NOTICE.

The stained scissors fell from her hand, clanging on the tile floor as they hit. The sound echoed as they bounced away from her feet. She was in shock, in spite of the feeling that the eviction was imminent. The man pulled a large stapled pack of papers from his briefcase and handed them to her.

"You've been officially evicted, young lady. You have until 5:00 P.M. to vacate the premises." He turned and took a couple of steps toward the door before stopping, turning, looking at the orange blood, and laughing an evil, spine tingling laugh. The man vanished beyond the door.

The people in the salon swarmed around Katrina.

Her former roommate Stevie chided her.

"I told you that you needed me to make this work. You need me Katrina. You've always needed me. Admit it. You need me . . . "

He was pushed aside by her boyfriend Jonathan.

"You can have her. I'm done with her anyways. It was fun while it lasted, kiddo, but seriously, me with you? This is what I get for playing below my class. I'm just glad I never introduced you to my mother. That would have been a horrible mistake."

Her lead stylist Kevin added his comments.

"I left my other job for this? I knew it was too good to be true. I should have known there was a reason you were so nice to me. You were never going to pay me, were you? I wish you were a dyke so I could slap you!"

Katrina stepped back, trying to get away from the pushing throng. She backed into her salon chair, where a hand grabbed her leg. It was Duncan, slumped over the side. He weakly called out to her.

"Help me Katrina . . . help me . . . "

Her other hairdresser Marlene pried Duncan's hand off of Katrina's leg.

"Never mind him. He's dead anyway. What about me? Trust me, you said. I know Toronto, you said. You'll take care of me, you said. Well you took care of me all right! Now I'm out of a job, with no money in a big city. I guess I can always become a prostitute to make ends meet."

Katrina started shaking and screaming, her arms flailing about.

"You're right! You're all right! I guess I'm just a stupid blonde from Pipton. I don't deserve to own my own salon. I'm not smart enough to run a business. I'm not outgoing enough to bring in new customers. I hate finances and couldn't balance the books if my life depended on it. I don't deserve a good boyfriend. I've got big feet . . . " She looked down and her feet were now covered in jumbo clown shoes, spattered in blood.

A distant voice responded to her, becoming clearer with each word.

"Wake up and stop hitting me. I'm trying to sleep." It was Jonathan.

Katrina sat up in bed. She was sweating profusely.

"Hold me Jonathan. You know I like to be held after I have a bad dream. More like a nightmare! Everyone was screaming at me and I had blood all over me. I was going to lose the salon."

She nestled up against Jonathan's shoulder, seeking reassurance.

"That could never happen, could it? I mean losing the salon?"

He rolled over and placed a gentle kiss on her forehead.

"No, of course not," Jonathan rolled over and put an arm around her. "Never."

Ten seconds later, he removed his arm and rolled the other way.

But it was enough to make Katrina feel safe again.

1 *Snow Day*

"Did I ever tell you that I hate this weather?" The view through the front window was a blur of giant white flakes. Kevin pouted as he watched the accumulation on the ground.

"No, Kevin, at least not in the past five minutes," replied Katrina to her obviously depressed employee. "Perhaps if you didn't spend the whole winter in R . . . I mean inside with Ron . . . you'd get some enjoyment out of all this snow."

Kevin turned his head and slowly rolled his eyes toward her. "That's easy for you to say, Darling. Heavy snow means no customers, which means no tips for Kevi-boy. You try surviving on what you charge me for my chair."

He had a point. But this *was* a new salon and you can't throw money away in the first few months — at least that's what Katrina's boyfriend Jonathan preached to her every month when he did the books. If it were up to her, she'd cut the chair rent a few bucks, but she wasn't the one with the business degree. Her idea of handling money was to hand it over to a cashier when she spotted a good bargain on a pair of shoes, and she seemed to find one of those about once a week.

"But tomorrow will be a killer for tips. We're always packed on the day after a snowy day like today, and everyone wants to share their snow disaster story . . . " Katrina barely got the words out her mouth before Kevin jumped in to finish.

"And when the lips are loose, so are the purse strings!" That thought seem to lift Kevin's spirits as he turned and pranced to the back of the salon.

Kevin wasn't your stereotypical gay hairdresser. While he certainly put on the airs, he was quite down-to-earth when you shared a pitcher of draught with him. He did like the occasional frou-frou drink, but that was mostly for show when out with Ron and his other gay friends. He'd rather have a nice cold draught any day, even if it had to be light beer. Kevin did dress nicer than your average straight guy, but was never over the top with outrageous colours or too much bling. A simple earring would do just fine for him, an understatement of his preferences.

Katrina had met Kevin through her ex-roomy Stevie. She had gone to Kevin for a cut only at Stevie's begging, which was pathetic to see, and what she interpreted as Stevie trying to please his gay friend. This was one of the many reasons that she had thought her former confidant Stevie was gay. Instead, Stevie had just turned out to be your run-of-the-mill live-in stalker type, deleting messages from would-be suitors for Katrina so that he could win her for himself. Not that Katrina had the least bit of interest in him. Stevie was so scrawny that he made

Kevin look fat, and Kevin likely tipped the scales at about 135 pounds. Katrina was thankful that she had kept Kevin's card from the visit to his former salon. When she told Kevin she was starting a new place and wanted him to become the feature hairdresser, he jumped at the opportunity.

It had been only a few months since Katrina took over the former Quick Cuts location and turned it into Kat's Kuts. She used the money from that house-wrecking "Life of the Party" final gig to start her dream business. She wouldn't have done it without the encouragement of her fellow PEST Cathy. The name of the salon actually came from her friend Cathy, who often referred to Katrina as Kat. It was amazing that she had known Cathy a few scant weeks while they were rented **P**arty gu**ESTS** (hence PESTS), yet this chatty wonder of a woman had transformed Katrina's life. She went from frustrated part-time waitress to owning her own hair salon, just like her mother, except Katrina's salon was in the bustling megacity of Toronto, while her mother's place was a few hours into the countryside in little ol' Pipton.

"Hey Katrina, do you think we can get out of here early today?" The request came from Marlene, the other full-time stylist that Katrina employed. Jonathan had recently suggested on numerous occasions that the salon didn't need three full-time stylists, but Marlene struck a chord with Katrina. Marlene too had come from a small town, and while she was certainly more confident and less shy than Katrina, she still likely felt like a fish out of water at times in T.O. Katrina had lived through this experience a few months earlier and really wanted to help her out.

"Yeah, sure, Marlie. We likely won't get two more customers all day. I'll keep Kevin around, just 'cause I know it will piss him off."

"I heard that." Kevin's voice came from the back near the storage room.

At that instant, the bell over the door rang (just like Mom's place), startling the three of them. In from the elements came a recognizable figure. That his name was Duncan was about all they knew about him. He must live somewhere nearby, because he came in every 3rd Wednesday at 10:00 A.M. like clockwork. They would occasionally spot him scurrying down the street, although he didn't look like he could possibly be going anywhere important. Duncan's clothes always looked like he had slept in them on a park bench for a few nights in a row. He didn't smell like a homeless guy, but his hair looked like he'd lost a fight for an acorn to a squirrel with issues. Duncan scared Marlene and he grossed out Kevin, so neither would cut his hair. Katrina liked him for all his quirkiness.

Duncan often never said a single word when he came in for a shampoo and cut. The silence creeped Marlene out, but Katrina saw a throwback politeness in it — almost Canadian to the extreme. Katrina also had an annoying habit, at least to Kevin. She had a way of always finding the good in someone or the best in a situation (refer back to the snowstorm outside).

"Hi, Duncan! Why don't you sit in chair two over there?" smiled Katrina as she gestured toward the half-turned chair in the middle. Duncan shuffled over to the chair and carefully sat down. Katrina couldn't help but notice the ever-present twitching in his hands and slightly shaky appearance of his legs. Marlene thought he was drunk and was barely holding it together. She half expected to mop up Duncan's vomit every time he came in, likely from consuming too much high-alcohol, over the counter cough syrup, or whatever the winos were using for a cheap buzz these days. She'd heard stories in her small town's Tim Horton's about the homeless in Toronto, and heeded her mother's warnings never to look them in the eye or it'd be just like looking at the devil. Although she didn't believe any of that devil nonsense, she did get anxious around the street survivors.

Katrina walked around Duncan, grabbed a cape from the counter, flipped it over his front, and then neatly tucked it in around his collar. As she reached for her comb and scissors, she heard the vibrating sound of a cell phone. Duncan wrestled with the cape and reached into his pocket, the source of the sound. The three stylists stared in amazement that Duncan would actually have a cell phone, even though Kevin had recently told them that Ron had seen one of the regular Queen St. "homeless" guys using one in an alley one day. Katrina was really irked by Kevin's story. She regularly threw those guys quarters and was ticked at the thought that she may have been paying some guy's cell phone bill instead of his lunch tab. Hell, she had just recently gotten one herself (and she still didn't know how to use it properly).

Duncan took a quick look at the phone and without looking up, tugged off the cape and got up from the chair, placing the clean cape over the arm of the chair. He simply said "Sorry," grabbed his crumpled coat from the rack and slipped back into the frozen tundra beyond the walls of the salon.

"Well, what was that all about?" said Marlene.

"I don't know," replied Kevin and continued with "and I don't care, but I'm never giving a homeless guy another dime!"

"I don't think he's homeless," responded Katrina. "After all, he's always paid me, although he's never given me a tip and he usually pays in loonies and other change."

"I always thought he was a freebie, since you're such a softie," shot back Kevin.

"I still think he's creepy — even if he's got a cell. Anyway, I'm outta here," concluded Marlene as she finished wrapping her wool scarf so that it covered her nose and chin.

2 *Waiting is the Hardest Part*

The next day at Kat's Kuts lived up to Katrina's billing from the day before. The place was buzzing all day, with all three chairs barely getting any free time, let alone the stylists working them. The small waiting area was filled most of the day, with walk-ins outnumbering the regular appointments. But through all of the waiting, nobody seemed to complain, not even about sitting on the frayed fabric on the waiting chairs that really belonged out back in the dumpster. The customers were all just happy they had survived another blast of old man winter, and were openly sharing their stories of yesterday's misadventures. What seemed like horrific events twenty-four hours earlier now became the source of humourous reflection.

Kevin could tell stories and chat it up with the best of them, and he was being put to the extreme test today. He was starting to lose his voice from the constant banter with the clientele, but was certainly reaping the rewards with the generous tips that were being forked over. Kevin recalled back to yesterday and how Katrina had called this one right on the money. He thought to himself that maybe she wasn't as naïve as she appeared. Regardless, this was one of his best days ever for tips, and he had booked a dozen future appointments from walk-ins alone. This made Katrina happy, as her mother had always told her that regulars paid the bills in the salon business.

While Kevin didn't want this glorious day to end, Katrina was watching the clock all day. She was anxiously anticipating the weekend. She was excited about going away with Jonathan for the weekend, but was unsure what a visit to his mother's cottage held in store for her. Even though they lived together, it didn't seem like they spent a lot of time alone. It seemed like the three-hour car ride alone with Jonathan would be the most time they had spent together at one time without having sex. She was just hoping that he wouldn't run out of things to say, forcing her to come up with interesting topics. She'd likely bore him to death talking about the salon. Jonathan got noticeably uncomfortable when Katrina went on about Kevin and Ron and how she was jealous of the relationship that they shared. And even though she'd heard at least a dozen snow stories today and a half-dozen good jokes, she'd never be able to retell them properly or get the same response as when they were told to her.

As 6:00 P.M. approached, the stream of customers slowed, as it typically did on a Friday afternoon. Marlene and Katrina found themselves both without a customer for the first time all day, as Kevin finished up a walk-in and had a regular just show up for her six o'clock.

"So, first time meeting the in-laws, eh?" quizzed Marlene.

"It's not in-laws until you're married, and it's just his mother. His father died years ago," replied Katrina.

"Too bad it wasn't the other way around. That means he's likely a momma's boy. And the fathers please more easily, especially when sonny-boy brings home a hottie like you," Marlene said as if she had written a book on the subject.

"Well, I already know he's a momma's boy," Katrina said, now fidgeting more nervously than before, "I think he goes up there every second weekend to visit her."

"I hear guys like that always mentally compare their girlfriends to their mothers, even if they don't realize it. They say that without knowing it they look for girlfriends very similar to their mothers in personality and looks," prescribed Marlene.

"Well, his mother must be a terrific person . . . and a hottie," snapped back Katrina, impressed with her own witty response. "But thanks for the inside scoop, Miss Freud."

"Just telling you what I hear, that's all. I don't put a lot of stock in that stuff. Heck, my last boyfriend's mother weighed more than one of our cows, and she was a mean bitch. And I'm not either of those, right?" she asked almost looking for confirmation.

But Katrina had lost track of the conversation by then, as she caught a glimpse of Jonathan in one of the mirrors and had turned and started toward the door.

"Hey, sweetie!" as she reached arms outstretched towards her roomy and boyfriend. She gave him a quick embrace and a peck on the lips that seemed to leave Jonathan a little short of the affection he expected.

"I thought six would never get here. Let me just take care of a few things and we'll get out of here. You did remember my bag, eh? Oh, I'm sure you did, forget I even asked. And did you gas up? And get cash? And hit the beer and liquor stores? You can tell me when we get in the car," finished Katrina, not taking a breath or even allowing Jonathan the opportunity to respond to any of the three or four questions buried in her rambling. She was showing her nervousness about the trip for the first time. At this rate, she wouldn't have to worry about starting conversation, just about stopping it before Jonathan drove the car off a bridge to end it all!

Katrina walked around to the cash register and started to empty what cash there was into a small, shiny silver bag. With everyone using debit cards and credit cards these days, there wasn't much cash aside from tips and the occasional old-schooler who didn't believe in or use plastic. And of course Duncan, who likely didn't have any cards to use. As usual though, her clumsiness got the best of her and most of the coins missed the bag, falling to the floor and bursting off in every direction across the salon. Some of them seemed to roll forever and into every corner of the place. "Damn it," she cursed, although likely not loud enough for anyone to hear her.

Marlene just stood giggling by her chair.

"Not nervous about the trip, eh?" although Marlene had seen Katrina do this on at least two other occasions without any apparent motivating distraction, just out of klutziness. "Don't worry about it Kat, I'll sweep it up like last time, and I'm sure Kevin won't mind brushing the hair remnants off."

"Thanks, Marlene. It's good to have something to look forward to!" Kevin quipped, still working on a client's hair.

Katrina took the bag, with the bills and coins that managed to find their way into it, and started to haul it to the backroom to store in the safe.

"Do you want me to take care of that, and drop it by the bank on our way up north?" queried Jonathan. "It won't take but a few minutes."

"No, but thanks. I just want to get going!" as Katrina tried to overcome her embarrassment and continued to the back to put it in the safe. "Just give me two minutes to freshen up," she hollered from beyond the wall. Jonathan looked around, and the dilapidated waiting chairs were now empty, so he plopped himself down, grabbing an old sports magazine from the table. He knew that Katrina never got ready for anything in two minutes and figured he had time to read a short article about something that happened two years ago. To his astonishment, and before he even selected which piece of history to pan over, Katrina emerged smiling and looking like a million bucks.

"Va Va Va Voom" was the sassy reply from Kevin. "You're almost enough to change a guy's mind looking like that."

"Really? You think so?" naively replied Katrina.

"No, not really. But enough to turn the head of every straight guy in T.O.," a teasing Kevin responded.

"It's true, Kat. You do look great! Have a good weekend at Mother's." Marlene couldn't help but throw one last dig in there, wishing she had a guy like Jonathan to take her to meet the folks.

"Never mind them, Katrina. They're right about how good you look, but they just wish it were them going away to a cottage for the weekend," defended Jonathon.

"Don't you wish, big boy?" quipped Kevin, knowing from Katrina how that sort of thing made Jonathan uneasy.

"Enough, you guys. Don't forget to close it up tight guys, and I'll see you on Monday. Have a good weekend, girls!" she finished, her back now to them as she followed Jonathan out the door, the tinkling door bell almost drowning out her last words.

3 *Mrs. Miller*

The trek back to the parking lot to Jonathan's car was a treacherous one. The guys paid to clear the lot obviously weren't the cream of the crop, as they usually did a shitty job. In the past, Katrina had seen them zip into the lot and finish their work in less than five minutes. They tended to navigate around any parked cars, burying the vehicles with the snow from the empty parking spots and aisles. Their methods resulted in drivers coming out to cars with hard-packed snow ploughed into their wheel wells, making it next to impossible to move the vehicles without digging the ice and crud from around the wheels. On this occasion, the ploughboys had done an even worse job than normal. It was obvious that they had done one very simplistic circle through the lot and left, dumping their load in its entirety on some poor sucker's car right at the entrance. And that guy likely thought he'd be easy-out, parking right at the entrance like that — a George Costanza parking spot gone wrong.

Jonathan slipped a couple of times, regaining his balance before coming even close to hitting the ground. You'd think these conditions would have Katrina sliding and falling all over the place, and that her natural awkwardness would lead to bruises and concussions from wiping out in a flailing grand display of limbs. But to the contrary, Katrina was very comfortable in ice and snow. It's as if she was part mountain goat when it came to that kind of weather. But, put her on a dry flat surface like a dance floor, and it was just a matter of time before she tripped over a line on the floor or the light coming from a strobe light. She often ruined a promising date by literally tripping the light fantastic. Her big feet were to blame for her clumsiness, she was convinced, but she couldn't explain how they acted like snow tires with chains on a day like today.

After reminding Jonathan to buckle up ('It is the law you know.') and likely sounding somewhat like his mother, they pulled away into the unusually light downtown traffic. The conversation was as sparse as the traffic. Katrina didn't know what to say without referencing the salon, or talking about what's going on in Kevin's life, or what Marlene's opinion is on x. So she remained silent, trying to come up with a topic she could broach. Jonathan meanwhile seemed lost in his own thoughts, paying attention to what little traffic there was.

Jonathan was indeed lost in his thoughts. This weekend getaway to Mom's cottage wasn't his idea. Well, actually it was, but not because he wanted to, but because he felt he had to. He'd been with Katrina a few months and in most ways it was a good roll he was on right now. She was an absolute knockout, the blonde, green-eyed beauty that stopped conversation when she entered a room. She got him into a lot of clubs and other doors that would have remained closed to him. Or, at least he would have had to stand in line like everyone else.

She was also that trophy kind of girlfriend to bring to dinner with business clients. If he had to come up with shortcomings for Katrina, he'd say her naivety in some situations and, compared to other girls he dated, her conversation skills weren't as strong. Jonathan had tried to cut off Katrina a couple of times when she was saying something that he thought was embarrassing, but found that pissed her off and made him look condescending in front of his clients. Before Katrina, most of his dates were business women who knew the business dinner routine, and were attractive women. Katrina, however, was stunning. Besides, there was something else about her that made him feel special when she was with him.

So when Katrina started asking the question that eventually comes up in all relationships, 'where is this going', Jonathan decided that a visit to Mom would buy him some more time. After all, what says serious to a girl more than meeting your parents? He had to keep the relationship going. Besides the obvious benefits of having a hot girlfriend, there was the money from her business . . .

"So, what are we going to do up there this weekend?" Katrina broke the silence and Jonathan's train of thought.

With the least enthusiasm imaginable, Jonathan replied, "Hang out, I guess. Drink Mom's booze. Drink more of Mom's booze."

"No really, what did you do with her all those weekends you were up there?" pressed Katrina.

"Drink Mom's booze."

"C'mon. What else? There's got to be something else!" continued the inquisition.

"Sometimes I headed over to the 'Last Resort' and paid for drinks. It gets busy on Saturdays sometimes," hoping this would get her off the topic.

"Do you rent movies, look at old photo albums, or talk about old times?" without taking the cue to ask about the 'Last Resort.'

"Okay. Sometimes we watch an old flick. Sometimes we play cards. And she likes Scrabble and doing puzzles. Happy now?" he rattled off, hoping she was.

"That wasn't so hard, was it? I didn't think you could just suck 'em back the whole weekend," she laughed.

"Wait until you meet Mom, and maybe you'll think differently."

"What do you mean? Does she like to party? I bet she drinks you under the table and that's why you're so tight lipped," she chuckled again.

"Yeah, sure. You'll see when we get there. So what else do you want to talk about?" he stated, with a sense of finality to the subject.

The rest of the car ride was just casual conversation. Katrina was able to keep them talking without touching on any of the taboo topics, and certainly without bringing up his mother again. Marlene was likely right. He was probably just a Momma's boy and was overly sensitive.

The time clipped by like the kilometers they covered, and soon they were slowly winding down the narrow snow-covered dirt road to the cottage. Fortunately, some vehicle with big tires had already packed down the laneway, so navigating it was fairly easy although not totally without a slip here and there. As the cottage came into view, Katrina half expected to see Jonathan's mother come running out to greet her baby boy. Jonathan brought their car to a gradual stop, maneuvering it so that they could pull out frontward on the way out. He worried about getting stuck later, if new snow fell.

"Well, here we are. I'll grab the bags and meet you on the porch."

Katrina grabbed the two pillows from the back seat and headed in. Jonathan wasn't far behind by the time she finished clambering over the seat, grabbing her purse, and spraying a quick shot or two of perfume on herself. Jonathan opened the door to the cottage for Katrina, and she entered, hugging the pillows close to her chest, as if in a defensive posture.

"Did you remember the KFC?" barked a voice from around the corner, likely in the kitchen.

"Oh yeah, I forgot it in the car," Jonathan replied apologetically.

"You'd forget your head if it wasn't barely attached," said the voice, now coming around the corner.

As Jonathan rezipped his coat and turned to retrieve tonight's dinner from the car, Katrina finally got to see his mother. Marlene wasn't too far off. Mrs. Miller was obviously once a very attractive woman. There was no hiding her fine features and clear skin. Even her figure was pretty good for a woman of her age. It was also obvious that she hadn't gone to much trouble today to get 'gussied up' for her son's visit. This was a surprise, as based on Marlene's portrait, Katrina expected Jonathan's mother to come to the door all decked out for her baby boy — no such case tonight.

Katrina put the pillows down on a chair by the door and draped her coat over the same chair. She bent down and unzipped her calf-high boots. As she moved the boots out of the way of the door, Jonathan's mom looked at Katrina's feet.

"Holy cow, those are big feet you've got there missy. If you were a man, I'd want to date you."

Her feet were a very sensitive subject for Katrina. She'd always been self conscious of their size. Katrina was already scared to death about this meeting and now her confidence had been shot down yet another notch.

As Jonathan returned, he closed the door behind him with his left foot and handed the bag with the bucket of chicken and poutine to his mother. "Here you go, Mom. Can we help you set the table?"

"Depends. Can I trust you not to break my good paper plates and plastic forks?"

Katrina thought it was funny and started to laugh. Then she noticed that Jonathan's mother wasn't smiling. Katrina was standing there in disbelief.

"What's the matter, Blondie? Too blonde to talk? Did you spill a bottle of cheap perfume on you or what? What's your name toots?"

"Katrina, ma'am," she whispered back, like replying to a teacher in the fourth grade when you know you're in trouble. The use of "ma'am" was also not a good move. You could see his mother's already pursed lips getting tighter; her glare almost brought her eyebrows together for an instant.

"Let's eat," Jonathon's mother simply replied, opening the bucket of chicken.

His mother started moving the pieces of chicken around with her hands, digging down to the bottom.

"You imbecile! You forgot to get crispy again, didn't you?"

"But Katrina doesn't like crispy," he defensively replied.

"Oh, Katrina doesn't like crispy. Can't Katrina eat fricken chicken any day of the week? I'm way up here craving crispy chicken and you don't bring me any."

Dinner was very quiet. Katrina was still in shock, while Jonathan apparently had no interest in opening his mouth except to scarf down chicken. Katrina picked at a single drumstick on her plate and swirled around some poutine in neat little circles, watching the little trails of gravy disappear behind it. In spite of her outburst before dinner, Jonathan's mother still ate three pieces of regular chicken. Mrs. Miller finished her meal and got up. No excuse me. No thank you. But the silence was the best sound out of her mouth so far.

"Do you play Scrabble, Blondie?" she asked.

"Sure. It's fun," a still cheerful Katrina answered.

"Sure. It's fun," his mother echoed, but with a nasally, whiney texture to it.

Jonathan rushed to finish the chicken on his plate. Although he really wasn't full yet, he knew better than to stay at the table eating. Fortunately, he loved cold KFC. He figured it'd taste even better later, following a quick hit outside after Mom headed to bed. Jonathan judged his weekends at home by the number of joints that he needed to medicate him to get through them. It was beginning to shape up as a ten jointer, based on the way dinner had gone.

The table was cleared and the game set up. Mrs. Miller grabbed a beer from the fridge without so much as offering one to her guests. Jonathan noticed the slight and got up and grabbed one for him and Katrina from the 2-4 he had lugged in earlier. He knew better than to come to the cottage empty handed. Maybe his sisters could get away with it, but not him. He'd still try to drink her stuff when she wasn't looking, because Mom bought the good liquor and he'd take the leftover beer home anyway. He placed the opened bottle of beer in front of Katrina and was about to sit down when he remembered she liked it with a glass, so Jonathan spun around and grabbed one out of the cupboard. Unfortunately for him, he wasn't paying attention and plucked a Toronto Maple Leafs glass.

"Friggin' Leafs!" cursed his mother. "I thought I told you to get rid of that damn glass last time you were here? Those shitheads do nothing but piss me off. The reason I play Scrabble and solitaire all the time now is because my doctor told me I had to stop watching those losing bastards. It was raising my blood pressure. Hell, I feel it now just talking about it."

Jonathan didn't say anything, but snatched the glass from where it was sitting and put it in the garbage. He then carefully took a non-descript glass from the cupboard and began to fill it with Katrina's beer, angling it just right so as to leave just a trace of head on the top.

"At least you can pour beer as good as your old man," grumbled his mother.

"Just the way I like it," a smiling Katrina replied.

"Funny, being a blonde I figured you'd like more head," snorted back the mother.

"Let's pick to see who goes first," interrupted Jonathan, hoping to change the subject quickly.

Jonathan managed to draw the lowest letter and got to go first. After rearranging his letters for a minute, he neatly placed the word JOB in the middle of the empty board.

"You couldn't come up with anything better than that to start the game? Maybe if you didn't have to mooch a job off your sister . . . " but she was cut off by Jonathan.

"It just so happens that I wanted to get rid of my J right away. It's your turn, Mom."

"B-I-T-C-H. Bitch. You're turn, dear," she turned and looked at Katrina with a Cheshire smile. Jonathan looked at Katrina apologetically, and Katrina mouthed back "It's okay," and turned her attention to her letters.

Katrina mixed her letters around for a few seconds, and then placed down the word HOBO.

"You mean like a tramp, dear? Of course you do. Your turn, Jonathan. Hurry up."

Jonathan fortunately was prepared and played the word ZOO. "I'm glad to get rid of that zed," he said, beaming that he achieved this feat so easily. His mother sorted her letters, and then looked at Katrina before placing down her word. "S-L-U-T. Your turn, Katie."

"It's Katrina, Mrs. Miller."

"Of course, dear," was the reply, implying it didn't really matter what her name was. And she certainly was implying what she thought of Katrina.

Katrina followed by playing the word SLEEP.

"Oh, that reminds me, dear. In case Jonathan didn't tell you, you two will be sleeping in separate rooms under my roof.

Jonathon lays down the letters for ORG.

"What the hell is an ORG?" growled his mother.

"It's short for organization"

"Well STUP, there are no short forms allowed at this table, so pick them up and make a real word. But I am impressed that you know a word with as many letters as organization."

Jonathan picked up the letters and sat staring at the ones in front of him.

"This could be a while," his mother said as she stood, picking up her empty and moving it to the counter. While she had her back to the table opening the fridge, Jonathan mouthed "I'm sorry" to Katrina.

"Still haven't played yet?" his mother kept up the onslaught as she turned back toward the table.

Jonathan placed down OGRE, and as he finished straightening the E, his mother pushed his hand aside and placed down the word PIMP.

"I'm sure you're familiar with PIMPS in T.O., eh sweetheart?" In a kind, motherly voice that contradicted the words coming out of her mouth, she added, "Have you ever met or worked for one?"

Katrina had about had enough by now. She knew she wasn't the sharpest tool in the toolbox, or shed or whatever the expression was, but she wasn't an airhead and certainly wasn't a slut. Sure she probably moved in with Jonathan way too soon after meeting up with him, but it was love, not a trick like his mother made it sound. She decided she had put up with enough of this and would start sending her own messages back across via the game board. She started to play the word LONELY. Before the word was completely laid down, and without allowing the mother to get a word in, Katrina said, "It must get lonely up here with your kids all gone and no friends around." This, of course, evoked a nasty glare from the mother, but no verbal abuse. That was refreshing to Katrina, impressed with her turn to the offensive. Inside, of course, she was shaking like a leaf, having summoned courage she rarely displayed. As usual, it took her getting really pissed off to find it. She had learned the hard way at a Life of the Party gig that finding bravery in booze didn't work too well for her; Jonathan's slacks also learned that lesson when she puked all over them.

This latest turn of events made the game more interesting to Jonathan. While he suffered through letters that would have challenged anyone and that forced him to play one or two letters every turn (how many words have the letter "I" in it four times?), he knew enough to keep his mouth shut and watch the battle rage on.

Jonathan hadn't seen this side of Katrina very often, and usually avoided her when she was like this because it was usually due to something stupid he had done to bring it out. He had never mustered much courage with his mother, and certainly felt that speaking up about anything was out of place. His father taught him that it showed respect to not talk back. Jonathan could swear that he could still feel some bruises deep down from the time or two that he had crossed the line and gotten the payback from his father. The odd thing though, as he thought about it, was that he ended up respecting his father and fearing his mother even though she had never so much as raised a hand in his direction.

The game continued with a level of intensity and passion not usually involved in a simple game of Scrabble. For the next thirty minutes or so, Jonathan's mother kept forming derogatory words that usually don't find their way onto Scrabble boards. She played EASY, WHORE, and HARLOT.

"HARLOT, - that's what we used to call a SLUT deary, in case you're not familiar with the word."

While Katrina's words were not quite so graphic or crude, she clearly made her intent known with HAG, MEAN, and GOAT. Jonathan was delighting in this silent battle of words, snickering under his breath on occasion, but hoping that neither of the combatants noticed. Unfortunately, he did not fly under the radar completely. His mother seemed to lose interest in picking on Katrina and started using words like MORON and LOSER, which he rightly assumed were directed at him. Katrina also detected this behaviour shift and backed off, playing more conventional words.

"Want a beer, hon?" Mrs. Miller said as she got up to get herself one.

"Sure, thanks," replied Jonathon.

"Not you, her," shot back his mother.

"Oh sure, okay. I'm sure Jonathan would like one too," piped up Katrina.

His mother didn't reply, but got three beers. She handed one directly into Katrina's outreached hand. She went around Jonathon's hand and partially slammed the bottle on the table. She'd never fully slam it during a game of Scrabble, as she didn't want to mess up the board.

Jonathan was finally happy when he got some consonants and was able to play SHIT. Katrina lunged forward and spit out some of her beer when Mrs. Miller scolded Jonathan for using a swear word! She thought to herself, *I guess SLUT, WHORE, and HARLOT are okay, so long as you don't use SHIT or DAMN.* And then to Katrina's further amusement, his mother put DIP in front of it to make DIPSHIT. This, of course, had worn thin on Jonathan by now, and he started a good five-minute argument about whether DIPSHIT was a word. Jonathan only conceded at Katrina's urgings, putting away the three dictionaries that he had scoured the living room for to back his point of view — all of which were irrelevant to his mother. She had made her point and delighted in finally getting a reaction.

Katrina wondered just what it was that Jonathan had done to earn all of this abuse from his mother. It certainly wasn't a "Momma's boy" treatment. What had he done in the past that his own mother showed him such lack of respect? Did his mother treat him like this every time he visited, or was this a special performance for Katrina? If this was the normal routine, why on earth would Jonathan come up here every couple of weeks? Did Mrs. Miller give him the guilt trip about visiting or something? It certainly didn't make sense to Katrina, but certainly not much surprised her anymore after living in Toronto for a few years. By now, Katrina just wanted to get the game O-V-E-R, and was glad when she was the first one to play her last piece.

"Done!" she exclaimed, half triumphant and half relieved.

"Well, I'll be! Katrina got lucky and went out first," replied his mother. Katrina sat with her mouth open. His mother had used her name and gotten it right. Katrina was expecting a crude reference.

"Fortunately, I was keeping score on the side over here, and I won by a landslide over you, and Jonathan's score was slightly above what a chimp would get. And he had all those high-point letters to start, too. What a waste. I don't think I can take playing another game tonight. It's too late and not much of a challenge anyway. Put the game away, eh? I'm hittin' the hay."

"Goodnight, Mrs. Miller," said Katrina in far too cheerful a tone considering what had happened in the game.

Mrs. Miller kept walking, her back toward them, and simply raised her hand slightly in silent acknowledgement. After his mother's bedroom door closed, Jonathan finally felt safe to speak.

"I think she just ran out of letters to make more terrible words aimed at you. Good thing I used the zed early, so she couldn't make SLEAZY. Maybe it is true what they say, that acting mean is more tiring than acting happy. She certainly looked tired."

"Yeah, I guess you're right. I've never seen a Scrabble board with SLUT on it, let alone on it twice like she did. So, what was that all about anyway?" wondered Katrina out loud.

Jonathan neither looked up, nor did he answer right away. He continued to put the Scrabble tiles into the bag one at a time, deconstructing the words along the way. It was almost like watching a fast rewind of the match. Katrina would normally have thought that this was odd, but after tonight, she didn't give it more than a few seconds of thought.

"Look, you've just got to tell me stuff for this relationship to work. It can't just be about sex you know," lectured Katrina, but in a caring way. Jonathan looked up, with an "it can't always be about sex?" look on his face.

"I know. I know. I just haven't ever gotten this far into a relationship before without screwing it up," he sheepishly replied.

"Well, you're going to hose this up if you don't at least try to explain some things."

Dale J. Moore

4 *Breakfast*

Daylight shone through the curtains of Jonathan's old room and slowly
progressed to the point of striking his face. He squinted and pulled the
covers over his head before realizing where he was. Then he really
wanted to keep the covers over his head. But he realized that Katrina
was probably already up and likely sitting in her room too scared to
emerge. He hung halfway off of the bed and stretched out trying to find
the clock under the pile of yesterday's clothes. He finally unearthed it
and saw it was 9:30 A.M. He hated getting up this early in the morning
on any day, let alone the weekend. He wasn't a damn farmer or baker.
But duty called, so he started to dig through the small bag he had
packed looking for clean clothes. Shit, he cursed to himself, forgot to
pack another pair of underwear. He thought of just throwing his pants
on without any, but had a vision of Ben Stiller in *There's Something
About Mary*. So on went yesterday's pair and a douse of cologne
directly onto them in case they were a little rank. He finished getting
dressed, but because of the way he packed, he looked like he had slept
all night in his fresh set of clothes. He took a quick glance in the mirror

to straighten his hair by hand, and thought 'screw it' to himself and moved toward the door. That's when he heard the laughing.

Katrina woke up around 8:00 A.M., feeling only slightly worse for wear from having a few beers the night before. At first she lay in bed wondering what today would hold for her. She was reluctant to venture out of her room for fear of running into Jonathan's mother alone. But nature was calling, and it was calling loudly. She opened up her neatly packed small travel bag and pulled out the clothes she had picked to wear today. Yesterday's clothes were taken from their neatly stacked pile and placed in the empty bag she had packed specifically to hold her dirty clothes. She got dressed and opened the door to the hallway. Katrina peeked out and saw the coast was clear so she scooted across the hallway to the bathroom, hairbrush and makeup bag in hand. Only a few minutes were spent on the basics before opening the door to head back to her room. After all, she was at the cottage and could always finish up later, if they decided to go somewhere. She dropped her hairbrush as she stepped out into the hall, and as she lunged forward to grab it, her lunge took her right into Mrs. Miller. They managed to hold onto each other as they bounced up against the wall. Katrina turned red all over, but was relieved that they didn't end up in a heap on the floor. Mrs. Miller was still in her 'granny gown', as Katrina liked to call the old-fashioned style fleece nightgown like her mother also wore.

"Well, good morning to you too dear! I'm not accustomed to dancing this early in the morning, and certainly not in my nightgown. I just put on a pot of coffee. Do you care to join me?"

Katrina wasn't sure if this was the same woman as the night before. Sure, Mrs. Miller had started to show some signs of kindness towards her by the end of the night, but it wasn't warm and hospitable like this morning's version. Perhaps, she had bumped her head on the wall when they collided. Whatever, she could certainly go for a hot cup of Joe and since the closest Timmy's was likely 10 kliks away in town, it would do.

"Sounds good. I'll just put my stuff in my room and come right out."

As Katrina entered the kitchen area, she could smell the welcome aroma of the coffee. Mrs. Miller had placed a little plate with a muffin at the spot opposite where she was sitting, apparently for Katrina.

"I hope you like blueberry. It's all I've got left. They're not homemade, but pretty good. Jonathan's sister brought them up last week. She got them from Costco. I usually eat half at breakfast because they're so huge."

Katrina looked down at the monstrosity in front of her, noticing it was a whole muffin. It had the circumference of a small cake. Did Jonathan's mother think that she could eat this whole thing?

"Just cut it in half if you don't want the whole thing," his mother said, noticing the look on Katrina's face as she stared down at the mega muffin. "I thought you might think I was cheap if I gave you a half muffin. I'm sure with your figure you don't eat much, so feel free to cut off what you want and I'll wrap up the rest for later."

"Thanks. I'll do that." Was that a compliment that she had just gotten? She definitely liked morning Mrs. Miller more than the one she had met the evening before.

"So, what do you guys have planned for today?"

"Don't know. We might head in to town to meet Jonathan's friends."

"I wouldn't waste my time, dear. They're all a bunch of lazy bums. I don't like my boy hanging around with those no-good goof-offs. They're just trouble, if you ask me."

"I thought he's known them since high school."

"Yeah, and most of them still act like they did in high school. Most of them didn't get through first year in university before dropping out. What a pathetic bunch."

"Or, maybe we'll go for a walk around the lake."

"Sounds like a much better idea. I used to love doing that with Mr. Miller. It's beautiful in any season. Some folks don't like going out in the winter. It's a stunning view on a day like today with that fresh dusting of snow overnight. There's something about it that just fills my soul with hope and warms my heart. I know some people think of winter as bleak, but I find it renewing. A walk is definitely a better choice than meeting up with the guys in town."

Katrina agreed, as before the weekend began she was dreading meeting 'the guys' as much as her boyfriend's mother. If the first meeting with them went anything like last night, she could certainly live without that experience. Katrina reached for her knife to cut her muffin in half. She didn't realize, however, that she had sat her coffee down on the blade of the knife. As she grabbed the knife, her coffee cup tipped over, spilling its hot contents all over the table. Katrina's hand sprung forward in an attempt to upright the cup, but she hadn't put the knife down first. This caused her to propel the mug off the table and send it smashing across the kitchen floor. She looked up terrified.

Mrs. Miller sat there, her mouth gaping open. Neither spoke for a good five seconds, which seemed like five minutes to Katrina. Then, Mrs. Miller burst into laughter.

"A bit of a klutz, are we? What do you do for an encore?" she said with a broad smile.

"I'll clean it up," Katrina stated, still rattled by the mess she caused.

"Leave it. It's not going anywhere. Well, except the coffee dripping on the floor, but we can get it later. So, any good stories about other mishaps, Katrina?"

"Well, misadventure does seem to follow me around. I was shopping the other day, looking for some gloves, you know, the heavy Thinsulate kind that would be good for walking around out here . . . "

"Where were you shopping at, dear?"

"At the Eaton Centre. I usually like to shop at the smaller places. They remind me of the shops in Pipton where I'm from. The prices are usually a little higher, but the sales people are almost always friendly and helpful, not the pushy, snobby, commission-based young girls in the malls. Anyway, I had just picked up a coffee at one of those small kiosks and was putting my wallet back in my purse as I headed up the escalator. I took a sip of the coffee and . . . "

"Let me guess, you spilled it."

"No, worse than that! The coffee made me feel warm, so with one hand I tried to take off my scarf and tuck it into my still half open purse."

"You mean one of those large bags that could hold two or three purses?"

"Yeah, that's the kind. With one hand I didn't stuff it in very well and the end of the scarf was still hanging out. So, I was going up the escalator as I was doing all this. I didn't realize it, but I must have lowered my bag to take a drink of coffee. I looked up just in time to see it was about two seconds until the end of the escalator. Well, I forgot about lifting up my bag, and my scarf started to get sucked up into the escalator where the treads roll into the end. I tried grabbing at it, but it was a big, bulky scarf and it wasn't moving — except further into the treads. Of course, I was panicking because I started to cause a pile up at the end of the escalator. I knew at that time that the scarf was a goner, so I let go and jumped off the escalator."

Mrs. Miller was laughing as she heard the tale and leaned forward with interest. "Then what'd you do?"

"So as I jumped away, I heard a horrible grinding noise and the escalator broke down and came to a sudden jerking stop. Bodies were flying everywhere. I just ran and got out of the mall as fast as I could."

"Say, I heard about that!" exclaimed Mrs. Miller

"What?" questioned Katrina.

"It had to be the same incident. Tuesday night, right?"

"Yes, but how . . . where?"

"It was on the news. You ever hear of Big Bob Baker, a lineman for the Argos? He's about 6'4" and 320 pounds — big, big guy with a very recognizable face. He does a lot of charity stuff, so he's in a lot of ads and interviews. He was on that escalator with you. They say he was facing backwards, signing some guy's hat as he was going up the escalator. So when you caused the thing to stop suddenly, he lost his balance and fell on the guy. His weight carried him and this guy down about eight to ten steps, wiping out some old lady too. Amazingly somehow she was okay, but the guy suffered a broken leg."

"Oh, I didn't realize. That's awful!" Katrina had always been klutzy at times, but she usually ended up hurting only herself and not other people.

"That's not the worst of it, dear. Apparently, now this guy is suing Big Bob Baker for the injuries, claiming he caused it by facing the wrong way and by not having at least one hand on the railing! I mean, he was the one who asked for the autograph in the first place."

"Maybe the guy's American or something. It seems they like to sue each other all the time."

"You'd think, eh? I guess he's working in Buffalo and was just back for the weekend. It must have rubbed off on him. I wouldn't tell that story to too many people if I were you. The jerk would likely come after you too."

They both laughed and exchanged smiles. Katrina realized that she was feeling at home, like sitting talking to her own mother.

"Funny, but you're the first person I've told. I guess I was just too embarrassed."

"Well, since we're telling embarrassing stories, I've got a good one to show you that you haven't completely cornered the klutz market."

"Go on. It will be refreshing to hear, Mrs. Miller," she encouraged her.

"Please, call me Debbie."

"Okay, Debbie," Katrina returned somewhat awkwardly.

"Jonathan's dad was a true romantic. He took me to South Padre Island for a getaway. You ever been there?"

"No. I hear it's a big spring break place."

"Well, it wasn't so much back a few years ago. Anyway, we went in September, so it wasn't an issue. It was a beautiful vacation. We spent the days on the beach or by the pool drinking pitchers of margaritas. At night, we had our fill of seafood and dancing."

"Sounds dreamy," said Katrina, visualizing her and Jonathan in their place.

"One night, we went to a place on the bay, or whatever it is separating the island from the mainland. It's like a mile wide and about five feet deep for much of it by the island. Any who, we had just finished a decadent meal of melt-in-your mouth lobster and steak, and they started up music on the deck. We headed out there to take a spin or two. So after a couple of faster songs . . . "

"I wish Jonathan would dance to the faster songs; he only likes the slow ones," piped in Katrina.

"He certainly doesn't have the grace his father had. Speaking of slow songs, one of our faves came on, so Tom led me out to the pier to dance in the moonlight reflecting off the bay. It really was like a movie; it was so amazingly beautiful and romantic. So I'm lost in the moment staring into his eyes, when I catch a heel in between the boards of the pier."

"So much for the romance," laughed Katrina.

"Oh, it gets better," laughingly replied Mrs. Miller. "So there I am trying to wriggle my foot loose in an effort to keep from spoiling this romantic moment. I'm using all my might to free myself from this trap. I decide that the best way to get the heel out is a sudden thrust forward with my knee. You know, try to power it out. At the same time, poor Tom decides to act gallant and kneels down to set his princess free."

"Oh no," exclaimed Katrina

"Oh yes. The shoe came loose and my knee went full force into his forehead, knocking him backwards. The blow stood him up straight for a split second, and then those gorgeous eyes glossed over. He fell flat on his back, unconscious into the bay. Tom was out cold. I screamed. Everyone on the deck looked over. So there he lay floating in his best suit. I'm standing there in my best dress. I freaked and jumped in after him. Fortunately, like I said, the water was shallow and warm. I dragged him out and he spent the next two days in bed with a mild concussion." She laughed heartily at the memory. "These things always seem funny later, don't they?"

"Thanks for making me feel better. I'm sure in 20 years the escalator story will seem funny too."

They both continued to laugh and didn't even notice Jonathan's entrance. They likely wouldn't have noticed him at all for the fun they were having, except his cell phone's Great Big Sea ring tone startled them both. Without saying a word to either of them, he flipped open the phone and looked at the number. He stared at it for a second, like he was just going to flip it back down and let it go to voice mail. Katrina could see him roll his eyes a bit and take a deep breath before uttering 'Yeah' into the phone and walking outside into the cold to take the call. Katrina looked at Mrs. Miller

"Likely one of the 'Lost Boys' calling to make drinking plans for tonight," she said to Katrina, with a definite sound of displeasure in her voice.

Katrina didn't know what to say. She did know that it was damn cold out this morning though, so she grabbed Jonathan's coat to take out to him on the porch. She threw on her coat and boots and opened the door. As she stepped out into winter, she could feel the rush of cold air into her lungs. No wonder people drink so much Timmy's in this country she thought. The porch wrapped around most of the cottage, and when she first came outside she couldn't see Jonathan. After a brief pause, she heard him talking around the corner to the left. She started toward his voice and couldn't help but overhear his conversation.

"Yeah, I know what I told you." Then a silence as Jonathan listened to the caller's response.

"I told you I'd get it to you next time I'm at the cottage. I'm stuck in T.O. this weekend and won't get there until next week." Again there was silence while the caller spoke.

"No need to get nasty. I told you my situation. I'll see you next weekend."

By now Katrina had quietly moved close enough to the corner that she could actually hear how loud the caller was talking back to Jonathan, although she couldn't make out what the caller was saying, just that he was obviously pissed at Jonathan. She heard Jonathan flip his phone down and utter "Shit" quietly. That was her queue to take another step toward the corner, and as she did, she ran right into him as he came around it heading in from the cold.

"Thanks, Katrina. Damn cold out this morning, eh?" wanting to get back inside, and assuming that she hadn't overheard anything. He grabbed the coat without putting it on and instead wrapped his arm around her shoulder and pulled her close for warmth as he continued toward the door.

As he walked in through the door, with Katrina beside him, he proclaimed to his mother "We're going home, Mom."

Katrina looked at his mother with bewilderment. This was certainly unexpected and seemed quite rude as they were his first words of the day to his mother.

"Good morning to you, too! Katrina, I'd offer for you to stay so we could continue our stories, but I'm afraid I couldn't possibly drive you all the way back to the city. I'm just not up to that kind of trip anymore."

Jonathan looked over at Katrina, giving her the evil eye. Katrina knew she had no choice but to head back. She'd seen Jonathan like that and witnessed his determination in these situations before. She knew that something was up and it wasn't good. He had just flat out lied over the phone to someone about not being at the cottage. Obviously, he didn't want to get caught in that lie and needed to get going. Katrina nodded to Mrs. Miller and was off to her room to quickly pack. Katrina was so organized that it took her only a minute to load up and have her bag in the kitchen. Jonathan, on the other hand, was disorganized but in a hurry apparently. As Katrina put on her coat and boots again, she noticed Mrs. Miller coming towards her.

"Have a safe trip, Katrina. Best breakfast I've had in a long time! Please come back some time and we'll pick up where we left off. It'd be nice to have someone visit and actually spend time with me."

"What do you mean?" Katrina asked.

"I'm afraid you'll have to find out for yourself, dear."

Katrina wasn't sure what she meant, but hugged her goodbye.

"Thanks, Debbie. It was fun."

Jonathan stood there in disbelief. Weren't these two calling each other names like troopers last night? He was convinced that he'd never understand women. Maybe this was their equivalent to two guys pounding on each other in a hockey brawl and then sharing a pitcher of draught in the pub afterward. Jonathan simply said 'Bye, Mom,' grabbed his duffle bag and his remaining beer as he went out the door, not even thinking to hold it open for Katrina. She followed a few strides behind, thinking the prick could have at least warmed up the car. She turned as she opened the door and returned a wave goodbye from her new friend.

"Debbie? What the hell was that all about?" Jonathan asked.

"When you tell me what leaving so suddenly is about, I'll tell you."

They drove home in silence.

Dale J. Moore

5 *Monday Blues*

The morning bus ride was unusually long today. Katrina was preoccupied in reflection about the weekend. She hadn't even noticed the couple making out two rows in front of her. Normally, she would wonder whether they were getting an early start, were on their way home from partying all night, or simply couldn't get enough of each other from the night before.

Today she didn't know if she should be angry with Jonathan or feel sorry for him. He had certainly acted like a jerk at times over the weekend, leaving his mother's cottage after only one night, and then stomping around the apartment for most of the rest of the weekend in some sort of adolescent hissy fit. And, he obviously had left out a few small things about his relationship with his mother that he should have told Katrina by now, based on how serious she thought the relationship had gotten. She was beginning to wonder if he was as serious as she was. Every time she tried to even come close to discussing their relationship, or his mother, he flailed his arms around and stammered like an idiot before leaving the room in a huff.

On the other hand though, his mother treated him pretty unmotherly, if there is such a word, she wondered. God, she thought to herself, am I still playing Scrabble or what? His mother did lighten up after a while during the game, and they were actually hitting it off in the morning before Jonathan announced he and Katrina were leaving. She was recalling Mrs. Miller's words when they were leaving and wondered what she meant by them. Jonathan obviously wasn't telling Katrina everything. Suddenly, she found herself shifting from sorry mode back to anger mode.

Katrina stumbled slightly getting off the bus, like she did most days. Unbeknownst to her, the regulars on her bus route looked forward to seeing Katrina exit the bus, not because they disliked her, but because it often led to humourous results. She had on a number of occasions miscalculated the distance to the curb from the last step on the bus, causing her to perform the equivalent of a blooper reel of missed gymnastics landings. Some days she'd snag her bag going out the bus door, resulting with her wrestling with it to get it free from the money box, driver's door release, or another rider's belongings. One time she had to run beside the bus for about 50 feet when her bag got stuck in the door. Fortunately, the driver noticed before he got the bus going too fast. She thought that the passengers were awfully nice when many of them gave her a standing ovation, but did find it a little peculiar.

Today though, she was just not paying attention and got off one stop too soon. Katrina thought that she could get to work in her sleep by now, but apparently she was wrong. As she approached the salon,

Katrina reached into her coat pocket where she had placed two quarters like she did every day. Although her mind was preoccupied with Jonathan, she did remember to drop her money into the hat that was placed in front of the bench where 'Spare Change' sat. Spare Change was the local homeless guy. He always sat on the same bench and would simply and politely ask all passersby 'Spare Change?', responding with a slight bow or nod and a 'God Bless' whether you donated or not to his survival.

"God Bless," as the coins tinkled amongst the dozen or more that already occupied a place in the hat.

As usual, Kevin had beaten Katrina into the salon and used his key to open up. While Jonathan didn't like the idea of 'that poofter having a key', Katrina was actually appreciative that Kevin was so punctual. She was grateful to come into a lit up salon. She always hated opening up on Kevin's off days. She felt safe in the area of town where the salon was located, but it still felt creepy in the salon with only a few lights on, especially in the winter when darkness hung around so late in the morning.

"Hi, Kat! Did you see Spare Change's new hat? It actually looks like a new hat, not like it's just new to him," an obviously caffeinated Kevin rambled before Katrina could even get her coat off.

"No. I missed my stop and really wasn't paying attention," she replied as she unwrapped her scarf on the way to the backroom to hang her coat.

Kevin sensed that Katrina wasn't herself. Katrina called it his 'gay spidey-sense' that gave him special powers to read people. Kevin simply attributed it to paying attention to people. That was his theory as to why gay men got along with women so well. He believed that gay men actually pay attention to women when they are talking, and are not too busy checking them out or trying to come up with the perfect line to help them score.

"What's the matter, darling? Tough weekend visiting Jonathan's mother? Let me get you a coffee and we'll talk about it before any of the 'payings' come in."

Katrina always appreciated Kevin and his thoughtfulness. She often thought that he was the perfect friend. He listened patiently and told her honestly what he thought. No strings. No manipulation like so many of her jealous women friends had pulled in the past. They would often tell her things to take advantage of her good nature and naivety, usually to get her to dump some guy so they could date him. Kevin had a mostly male perspective on things, and she never had to worry about his hormones affecting his guidance to her.

He brought the coffee out from the back and sat down opposite her, sitting feet flat on the ground, legs close together, and hands on his knees leaning forward. It was an extremely gay-looking pose, but Katrina had gotten used to it and no longer chuckled under her breath at it.

Without holding any punches, and showing his dislike toward Jonathan, he blurted out "What'd the prick do?"

Katrina didn't like to kiss and tell, but this weekend certainly didn't involve any kissing, so she guessed the telling was okay.

"I just don't feel I can trust him right now," she answered quietly, almost embarrassed by her remark.

"Oh, dear. I think I should have skipped the coffee and just given you tequila. Those are never good words for anyone to say about their partner, gay or straight." Kevin reached forward and gently placed his hand on her knee as he spoke.

Just then they heard the tinkle of the door chime and in walked Marlene. Seeing the closeness of the two and Kevin's hand on her knee, she couldn't resist teasing him.

"You're not changing teams on us now are you Kevin?" followed by a light chuckle from her that caused Kevin to quickly withdraw his hand from Katrina's leg.

"Never without notifying you first sweetie," Kevin replied, getting up to take Marlene's coat. "We were just about to discuss Katrina's lousy weekend. What's new with you?"

"Say, did you see the new hat God Bless had today?" Marlene replied, not really catching the part about the lousy weekend at first and responding to the new part of Kevin's comment. Marlene was also a sickening optimist at times. She thought of it as 'reflecting on the positive'. This was the reason she referred to 'Spare Change' as 'God Bless', preferring to ignore his homeless status and highlight how polite he was and grateful for what the world handed him every day — or, at least what the world put in his hat every day.

Realizing finally what Kevin had said, Marlene held her other comments about 'God Bless'.

"Did you say Katrina had a lousy weekend? I was right about the momma's boy thing, wasn't I?"

"Yes, I did say she had a bad weekend. We just got started. Sit down sisters and let's get to it."

But before they could all sit down, a noise at the door had them all turning in sync to the front of the salon. Through it came a well-dressed man carrying an over the shoulder laptop bag. He turned smartly and closed the door firmly behind him. Without saying a word, he carefully stomped his Italian-made dress shoes to remove a few scant traces of snow. He didn't look like their typical clientele, but more like one of Stewart Windle's executive business acquaintances. Stewart was the brains behind the Life of the Party gig that had landed Katrina the money for this place, and he was well connected in the business community. Stewart dressed like a classy, well-heeled gentleman. His British accent added to the illusion. He came off like David Niven in an old movie.

The gentleman at the door left his coat on and took two steps toward them. He could only see Marlene and Kevin, who were standing up blocking his view of a sitting Katrina.

"Katrina . . . ?" he questioned in a very unsure tone of voice.

"Sorry, wrong girl," Marlene replied checking him over from head to toe, while slowly turning to the side to reveal Katrina sitting down behind her.

"That's me. You must be a friend of Windle," she assumed out loud.

"Don't know a Wendle," and he paused to look closely at Katrina before he continued, "Of course, the green eyes. That's why I hesitated with the other one."

Katrina thought that was an odd response, but didn't say anything.

"I'm Mr. McAllister's legal representative," He spoke much more confidently this time.

"I don't know any McAllister. Do you guys?" she turned with a lost look on her face. Both Marlene and Kevin silently shrugged their shoulders, looking as puzzled as Katrina.

"He was a regular client of yours," the lawyer replied, trying to clear up the mystery, but not providing enough information to do so.

"What do you mean 'was'?" injected Marlene.

"Unfortunately, Mr. McAllister passed this weekend," he replied.

"Passed what?" asked Katrina in a naïve way.

Kevin kicked her and whispered "Passed on. Died. Kicked the bucket."

"Oh, I'm sorry . . . but are you <u>sure</u> you've got the right salon? Brash Cuts is just two doors down. You seem more like their kind of clientele, the kind that doesn't mind paying $50 for a wash and cut," she responded, noting his expensive suit, likely Hugo Boss or the like. It probably cost the guy more than she paid for two month's rent and food.

"Quite sure, Miss. Mr. McAllister mentioned the place and you by name. He described you to a tee. He came in every third Wednesday like clockwork. He was very structured in his ways."

"You mean Duncan?!" Kevin blurted out.

"Yes, of course. Duncan McAllister. Who did you think I meant?"

"Well, certainly not Duncan" replied Marlene. "I mean nothing personal, but he looked like the type that only needed a lawyer to bail him out after a street sweep of the drunks."

"You shouldn't speak ill of the deceased, sweetie. It's not good karma," a worried Kevin cautioned her.

"Duncan's dead???" a stunned Katrina finally acknowledging it as she stared off into space toward the corner of the shop.

"I'm afraid so, Miss. His illness finally overcame him. He fought so hard for so long. It's too bad really. He was such a bright man."

"His illness? We had no idea," Katrina replied, looking at the others and sitting down again. "I guess that explains the nervous twitches and why he wasn't so stable on his feet."

"And I thought he was a drunk," an apologetic Marlene said, almost whispering her words out of shame.

"But why are you here?" posed Kevin to their visitor.

"One of Mr. McAllister's, I mean Duncan's, last requests was that Katrina style his hair for his funeral," he stated, in a straightforward manner, like they should have known that.

"WHAT?" they all bellowed out at once.

"He said that Katrina was the best stylist that he'd ever had, and that she treated him normal, not like some freak," he paused briefly and looked at Marlene " . . . or homeless guy."

Marlene and Kevin looked down at their shoes, embarrassed by their reactions to Duncan previously when he had dropped in.

Looking up, Kevin said, "I don't know. The thought of cutting a dead guy's hair creeps me out," he said in an almost pleading voice.

"I'll do it," replied Katrina without further hesitation, and with not really giving the whole dead thing much thought. She just knew it was the right thing to do.

"Good. He'd be pleased. He's at Shady Rest. I've already talked to the director over there and he's expecting you between 4:00 and 6:00 P.M. today. His name is Mr. Better. Seems like a right proper gentleman," he finished. He nodded to Katrina, and turned toward the door before turning back again and saying "Oh, by the way, there's $500 in it for you. Good day. It was a pleasure meeting you." And out the door he went.

"Five hundred bucks! Maybe working on a dead guy wouldn't be so bad. Do you need some help?" Kevin anxiously inquired, forgetting his earlier willies about it and thinking more about maybe getting a chunk of the cash if he helped.

"What will you do to help? Keep the dead guy from flinching during his haircut?" sarcastically replied Marlene.

"Stop referring to him as 'the dead guy'. His name was Duncan. Show some respect!" Katrina raised her trembling voice as she turned and ran to the back crying.

"Nice going!" Kevin glared at Marlene.

"Bitch," Marlene glared back.

6 *Shady Rest*

Katrina once again sat forlornly on the bus. This time she was lost in thought about the mysterious Duncan McAllister, whose last name she didn't even know until a few hours ago. It certainly took her mind off of her problems with Jonathan. Death has a way of making life's problems seem less important.

She had never gone to the Shady Rest funeral home, but couldn't imagine that any of them were much different. Katrina had never seen behind the scenes before though, so to speak, and this made her a little nervous. Hell, she'd never touched a dead body before and now she was going to cut hair on one. And not just any dead body, but someone that she knew and liked.

After getting off the bus, at the right stop this time, she made her way up the long walkway to the funeral home. It looked a bit more modern than the other ones she'd had the misfortune to visit in recent years. The funeral home had a White House look going for it, with pillars and new-looking siding on it. There was even a little white wrought iron fence around the front. She didn't know whether this was some tacky rip off or purely unintentional. Either way, it made her smile at the sight.

She wasn't sure whether she should go in the front door, or some back entrance for the workers. She decided the front was the best choice, not knowing any one and not wanting to be confused for a burglar. Do funeral homes have burglars, she wondered? What would they steal — did people sniff embalming fluid to get high? With that peculiar thought still in her head, she opened the oversized front door and entered. Inside was the usual foyer, with doors appearing in all directions. A few of the doors obviously led to visitation rooms, and she could see a small bathroom tucked in one corner. Another door was partially open, and looked like it was the office. There was a nice, but fake flower arrangement on a table between a few of the doorways. In a corner stood an odd statue of an elderly gentleman dressed in a 1940's style suit. She wondered if it was a tribute to the founder of the place or something, because it certainly wasn't adorned with a handsome face like you see on most mannequins.

Katrina took a couple of cautious, uncertain steps towards the partially open door, and then craned her neck in an attempt to see into the slight opening.

"Can I help you young lady?" came a low, cracking voice.

She was startled, not having seen anyone in any of the doorways. She turned to see the statue had come to life, at least barely. It hadn't moved from its original placement, but had turned one foot and done a very slight pivot to face her. She leaned toward it, grimacing to see any sign of life. The man-statue's skin colour gave the appearance that he'd already been embalmed.

"Uh, yes, I'm looking for Mr. Better. Is he in there?" and she motioned to the office, still trying to detect any movement to ensure she wasn't talking to a wooden figure.

"Yes Miss, he is. Shall I get him?" he replied.

"No, that's okay. I'll just knock on the door," answered Katrina, thinking to herself that it would likely take him about forty-five minutes to move across the foyer to the office at his pace. She was hoping to be out of here by then and back on the bus.

"Excuse me, Mr. Better?" Katrina called out as she gingerly tapped on the door, nudging it barely further open in the process.

"Come in, please," the voice beyond the door came back.

"Hi. I'm Katrina. I'm here to do Duncan's, I mean Mr. McAllister's hair for his funeral," still trying to grasp the concept.

"Oh, sure. Right on time I see," he replied pointing to his Rolex as he stood up. He got up from his deeply padded leather chair at the same time that she came forward. As she entered the room, he gave her the usual awestruck look that most men give her upon first meeting. Even in a somber place like this she looked striking. He was an average looking middle-aged man, with a few touches of grey beginning to make their presence known on his reasonably full head of hair. The nice suit and the dabs of grey made him look the part of a conservative funeral home director. He was just what she expected.

"Have you ever worked on a deceased person before?" he inquired, very politely and sounding concerned for her well-being.

"No, can't say I have," she answered, slightly biting her lip out of concern. "Any words of advice?"

Mr. Better was still registering the last sentence, his male hormones stuck on the image of her biting her lip, like some beer-girl in a commercial.

"Ugh," clearing his throat, "Uh, I mean no, except I suggest I escort you back there, as it can shock you the first time you step into the work area. We've had our share of fainters over the years." He had started to sit again, but abandoned that and stood straight up, buttoning up his suit coat in the same motion.

"After me, please," as he walked past her and into the foyer. "Hello, Granderson," he said as he passed the elderly man guarding the foyer. Granderson nodded slightly, again barely exerting enough energy to be presumed living. Katrina's eyes stayed on him most of the way through the foyer, to the point of almost losing Mr. Better and heading through a wrong door.

"Call me Ben." Mr. Better turned to Katrina, not noticing she had strayed slightly.

Ben Better? Katrina kept an inner chuckle to herself. She thought that all of his clients had 'been better' too. "Sure, Ben," she replied politely as she followed him down a stairwell at the back of the funeral home.

He stopped at the door at the bottom. "Are you sure you're okay with this?"

"No. But let's go," trying to convince herself to act bravely.

They walked into a fairly sparse, bright white room, with what looked like an operating table in the middle. It had some funky looking straps and handles on it, although Katrina couldn't figure out why you would need to hold the body down, like she had teased Kevin earlier. It's not like it's going anywhere on its own. There was a cart off to one side that had what looked like a blender on the top of it, and tools on a lower shelf. There was no sign of a freezer for the bodies, like she had always imagined.

Ben went into an adjoining room and wheeled Duncan's body out into the embalming room. "He's all ready, except he needs to get dressed after you're done. I mean I have to dress him once you're done. There's a head block under the table to prop his head up, if you wish. And on the side wall there's a small sink with a wand you could use to wash his hair" as he pointed to the left, "along with some clean towels, and styling tools."

"Okay, but I brought my own stuff, just in case."

"All right, then. I'll leave you to it," and he gave her a tentative pat on the back and headed out of the room.

Katrina stared at the body of Duncan. He was simply covered in a hospital type blanket. Below him on the operating table was the head block, and beside it lay a small box labeled 'personal effects'. Curious, Katrina bent down to take a peek. Of course, she accidently hit the table on her way to bending down, and Duncan's arm fell off the side and hit her in the head. She almost jumped out of her skin. She carefully put his arm back on the table. I guess that explains one reason for the straps she thought. She bent down again, this time more carefully, and pulled the personal effects box up onto the table to look at. She opened the box to find a nice Gucci watch, likely worth over a thousand bucks. Not a Rolex, but not bad for a guy she thought was homeless. She also found a gold chain, with a small gold pendant in the shape of a computer monitor. There also was an old, antique-looking pocket watch that was likely going to decorate his suit coat pocket. This was assuming that he had a suit, as she had only ever seen him in wrinkled casual clothes.

Katrina put the items back in the box and returned them to their spot on the lower level of the table. She rolled the table over to wash his hair. As she pulled back his blanket slightly, she was slightly grossed out by the marks near his collarbone where they had cut into him to do the embalming. Catching her breath and the vomit coming up her throat, she put the head block in place and went to work. She had many non-talking customers in her business, and Duncan was usually one of them, so she just pretended it was just another time cutting his hair. For some reason, the song 'If I had a Million Dollars' came into her head, and she sang it to herself repeatedly until she was done, one time changing the words to say "If I had a million dollars, we wouldn't have to cut hair, but we would, but not on dead people though."

7 Job Offer

Katrina wrapped up the tools of her trade and put them back into her oversize purse. She headed up the back staircase to find Ben so he could put Duncan back wherever he was supposed to go. Upon reaching the last step, she reached for the knob on the door that isolated the downstairs work area from the funeral home proper. As she did, the door was opened by someone on the other side, causing Katrina to fall on her elbow and bang her knees on the top step. The contents of her huge purse exploded across the polished hardwood floor above. She looked up to see the legs of a woman. One of the ladies' black pumps was covered in red nail polish, which had unfortunately broken as it flew free from the depths of her purse. Katrina followed the legs up to a thirty-something woman, who had an appalled look on her face.

"I'm so sorry," Katrina said, at first reaching between the ladies' legs to retrieve a tube of mascara, then starting to crawl around beside them to fetch other wayward objects.

"Oh, you klutz!" the lady half screamed, remembering at the last second where she was, halting in mid thought a full-frontal verbal assault.

This was obviously not the first time that Katrina had the klutz label slapped on her, but the first time in a funeral home, at least as far as she could remember.

"I said I was sorry," she said, "and I know how to get that off of your shoes."

"Never mind. They're just cheap hundred-dollar shoes," replied the woman, truly not concerned with the shoes.

Katrina was hoping the lady would throw them out in the nearby garbage. She wasn't above going into the trash to pluck them out and clean them up. They looked about the right size, and while $100 may not be much for this lady to spend on a pair of shoes, it was for Katrina.

"You must be Katrina" the lady said as she held her hand out to help Katrina up off the floor. "My name is Tammy. Tammy Parker. I'm Ben's assistant. I mean the assistant director, not his administrative assistant."

"Oh, sure. Nice to meet you. I was just coming up to find Ben to . . . " as she leaned forward to whisper as she looked around. " . . . to put Duncan's body back properly. I wouldn't want him thawing out or anything." As Katrina stepped back to hear a response, she looked closely at Tammy for the first time. Tammy looked about 5 foot 4 inches, in stained heels, so likely about 5 foot 1 inch based on the heel height. Tammy wasn't overweight, but she wore her clothes a little too tight, showing a bit of a roll around the waist. She also was showing a lot of cleavage, which didn't seem appropriate for an assistant funeral director, even if she was donning a black dress. That Katrina could tell Tammy was wearing a lacey black bra also seemed wrong.

"I'll take care of that Katrina. Besides, he won't thaw. He's been embalmed so no refrigeration required. Ben wants to see you in his office," and Tammy paused to look around " . . . after you pick up this mess. And tell Ben to get one of the guys to clean up the nail polish that missed my shoe." Tammy scooped a couple of tissues from a nearby box and dabbed at the damaged shoe briefly. She straightened, and then gingerly made her way through the clutter to the trashcan, before proceeding down the stairs.

Katrina navigated her way back to the front of the building where Ben's office was located. She said hello to Granderson as she walked by. This time the door to Ben's office was wide open. He sat at his desk doing some paperwork, not noticing her entrance right away. As he did notice, he stood up beaming at the sight of her.

"You did very well, Katrina."

She looked puzzled. He hadn't gone down there since she started, and Tammy couldn't have reported back that quickly.

Noticing the look on her face, he continued "Cameras. I was watching you on the cameras we have down there."

"Oh," said Katrina, now feeling somewhat violated instead of puzzled.

"I didn't get a good look at your work, but I was impressed with how well you handled yourself. You didn't seem skittish at all."

Obviously, the camera didn't catch how she was feeling.

"I was a little nervous, but it wasn't as bad as I feared," she replied. It wasn't as bad, but it didn't mean that she enjoyed it either.

"So you'd consider doing it some more?" he stated more than questioned, also seeming pleased with himself.

"What?!" a startled Katrina said.

"Mr. McAllister's lawyer said that you'd consider the job offer."

"What job offer?"

"Oh dear," he said sitting down. "I'm so embarrassed. He told me that if you handled cutting Duncan's hair okay that you'd listen to my offer. I suppose it was just a trick."

Katrina felt badly about it too, not that she had reason to, but because it was just the way she was brought up to put herself in the other person's shoes. "What's the offer?" she asked, regretting it the moment the words came out. She should have just gotten out of there. She convinced herself, *Fine, you were polite and asked, but you do not have to say yes. Don't let yourself get manipulated Katrina.*

"Well, normally a director or intern from the funeral home just does the hair, but Tammy has carpal tunnel in her right wrist. I have arthritis, and I really wasn't good at it anyway. Our two other directors just left for a long vacation to New Zealand. So I called a couple of stylists but they thought I was a crank caller. Besides, it's not most people's cup of tea, you know. I only need someone for about a month, part-time. Sure, we're busy, but not everyone needs a clip before moving on. I can give you $75 per person, which will have to cover your travel expenses here. But, I can't guarantee you a certain number of jobs a week."

Katrina had actually talked herself into saying no, at least a Katrina no, which came out as "Can I think about it for a few days?" While the job didn't appeal to her, the per person rate was a lot better than the $15-$25 basic rate she charged at her own place. It could mean some new shoes.

Having not gotten any stylist even this close to potentially taking the job, Ben stood up quickly and used both of his hands to grasp one of hers. "That'd be great! Let me get down your number and I'll check back with you in a few days." Ben gave her two of his business cards. "Keep one for yourself, and write your number on the back of the other one for me." As she wrote the number to the salon down, Ben added "Now I believe that Duncan's lawyer is paying you for today, right?" making it clear to her that he wasn't forking over $75 today.

"That's right," she agreed. "One more thing though. Why do you have cameras around the funeral home?"

Deciding that the truth was not the best course of action in this case, Ben responded "We've had some burglaries in the past, so I had them installed." He was hoping that he wouldn't have to explain further.

Not wanting to seem naïve, Katrina didn't ask for further details.

"Thanks," Katrina said, holding up his card as she looked toward the door.

"No, thank you," Ben replied. "I'll call you in a few days. I'll have Granderson get your coat."

"No bother," she quickly replied, wanting to get her coat before summer when she'd have no need for it.

Katrina exited Ben's office and headed toward the foyer coatroom when she stopped dead in her tracks.

"Cathy!" she exclaimed with the excitement of seeing a long lost friend. About a month and a half had only passed since they had met for drinks to catch up on the salon and each other's love lives. Cathy had been seeing someone, but in very unCathy-like fashion didn't want to talk much about it. Katrina thought maybe she had gone on so long about how great Jonathan was (at the time anyway) that maybe Cathy was embarrassed that her guy wasn't as terrific. Cathy had simply said though that things were going better than most of her relationships, and didn't want to jinx it by talking about it.

Cathy turned to Katrina, certainly not expecting to see her at the funeral home.

"Kat? What are you . . . did you know Blake Johnson?" referring to the deceased residing in the "Blessed Angels" room of Shady Rest.

"Who? No. I was here to cut a former client's hair, Duncan McAllister."

Cathy stepped forward and gave Kat a big bear hug. "So glad to hear that hon," releasing her grip. Cathy moved over to the guest registry book and signed 'Helen Smithson-Johnson', put the pen down, and proceeded to take her coat off. She noticed Katrina giving her 'the look'.

"I'll explain in a minute," she whispered and winked.

Katrina left her coat hanging in the coatroom and followed Cathy into the back of the room hosting Mr. Johnson's funeral. Cathy wasn't a knockout like Katrina, but dolled-up pretty well for such occasions. She was very outgoing and Katrina was envious of that attribute. Cathy knew how to liven up a place, even a funeral home, and dressed to draw attention to her best and biggest attributes.

"Before you judge, listen up. Remember Life of the Party? Of course you do. That's where we met. Well, Stewart . . . "

"I knew Stewart was involved when you wrote that fake name."

"And I told you not to judge so quickly. Well, Stewart found that the Party business was a little too messy, what with the crashers and thieves trying to move in on his deal."

Katrina was well aware of the problems that Stewart encountered with Life of the Party. She was embarrassed later to have to tell Cathy that one of the burglars was her creepy, night prowler ex-roommate Boris. She listened as Cathy continued.

"But his rich, lonely friends still had money to throw around. What Stewart found out was that the parents of these friends had reputations to maintain, even in death. The wealthy want to go out with a splash, I guess. It is their one last chance to impress everybody. So, the kids and spouses started paying Stewart to arrange for crowds of people to attend funerals of the deceased."

"That's awful!"

"Yeah, and you just cut a dead guy's hair. And it's not awful. It's a tribute. We're providing a service. Don't you want a lot of people at your funeral?"

"I haven't really thought about it."

"Well, I have. You know how much I love a party, with a lot of good stories and laughing and drinking. That's what we provide. We send them over to the other side in style. And the sons, daughters, and spouses pay handsomely indeed. After all, they look at one of these funerals as a social barometer, like how many people you have at your wedding and how outlandish it is."

"But you don't even know them."

"Same gig as a PEST Kat. Stewart gets cover stories for us. We usually get a couple of funny anecdotes to tell, and we circulate through the crowed telling them. Hell, we make these people's lives better than they ever were! Stewart calls his business 'Friends of the Deceased'. He calls us FREDS this time around.

Katrina glanced around the room, wondering how many of these FREDS were in the room. She thought she recognized a couple of faces, assuming they were also former PESTS, but her shyness made her lousy with remembering names or faces. Besides, they weren't allowed to socialize with other PESTS in Life of the Party, so she never got names or even knew who was a hired guest at the parties.

"Say, did you say how you knew that McAllister guy? I think we're FREDDING his funeral tomorrow."

"I doubt it. I don't think this guy comes from money."

"Maybe not. Could have the name mixed up. Well, I better get to work," Cathy said, pushing up her bra at both sides to pump up the cleavage. "There, that'll draw some attention. I'm the long lost sister-in-law, sort of the trampy widower of the deceased's brother. Rumour has it that he and I had a fling years ago, before his wife passed away. The son wants to piss off his mother's relatives one more time, before they find out they get none of the estate."

"That's harsh!"

"Should be fun!"

"Sounds like something that you can pull off," Katrina laughed. "How 'bout we catch a drink tomorrow night and you can tell me what happened?"

"Great. Call me!" and off to mingle and stir it up went the temptress Helen.

8 Stewart Returns

"Hello Stewart, honey. It's your mother."

Stewart had seen his parent's phone number come up on his cell phone many times in the past few months. He'd always let it go to voice mail. The first few times his mother left messages, and although she kept calling, she gave up leaving messages after the first few times. Stewart was fairly certain it wouldn't be his father calling, but was worried that it would be bad news.

"Hello, Mother. How's Toronto these days?"

"Getting colder by the day. Thank god for the theatre to relieve the gloom."

"That's you, Mother. Always looking on the bright side of life."

"Speaking of which, I talked to your father about your recent affairs."

Stewart's heart dropped in his chest. This was the reason he dreaded answering her calls. Life of the Party had been a reasonably successful venture financially for him, especially since it was a *legitimate* business. He'd abandoned a good chunk of money in his haste from that last disastrous party, but it was worth it to get out of there before being bludgeoned by a PEST that was looking for their back wages, or worse yet being arrested. There was after all the trust fund to protect, and a police record would have given his father ammunition to take that away.

"Go on, Mother."

"Well, I was able to convince your father that your business entrepreneur skills were to be lauded, not criticized. Just because, what was it called, Life of the Party? . . . I told your father that just because it wasn't a traditional brick and mortar setup like he is used to financing, doesn't mean it was reason to punish the boy. I mean you. I told him that it could be a lot worse, and it's not like our son is a con man or a drug dealer."

If only she knew his past, Stewart thought. But his wheeling and dealing in Montreal did not catch up with him in Toronto, aside from that punk using it to blackmail his way into a job that eventually brought down Life of the Party.

"Thank you, Mother. You are a blessing and a visionary." After saying that, he hoped he wasn't pouring it on too thick.

"Thank you, son. If only your father recognized that sometimes."

"I'm sure he does, Mother. You know how nonexpressive he can be."

"Yes I do, except when he's talking about you and that trust fund. But don't worry, he hasn't spoken of that in a few weeks, besides assuring me that he has backed off and isn't pursuing any changes to it."

"Thanks again, Mother."

"So when are you coming home, dear?"

"I'm not sure, Mother," he replied truthfully. "But it likely won't be too much longer."

"That's good to hear son. Just don't wait to let us know you're in town like last time."

"Yes, Mother. Love you."

"Love you too, son. See you soon!"

Stewart was beaming with the news of his 'pardon' by his father. He was relieved, mostly to hear that his trust fund was intact, but partly because his luck had been running out, along with his stash of cash.

He had relocated from the resort to a smaller, somewhat seedy hotel as a result of his financial depletion. Stewart had been tempted many times to stray from his new path on the straight and narrow. The islands offered many easy targets. When his wallet began to thin out, he started scouting opportunities, as he called them, for something that could replenish his pocket book and that he could justify in his mind as legal, more or less. Just in case, he kept a list of other less than legal opportunities too; it's important to have a fall back plan he reasoned.

To celebrate his mother's call, Stewart went to dine at a fine restaurant across from the resort he had abandoned. As fortune would have it, when his luck changed, it changed fabulously! After dinner, he pulled up a seat at the bar and ordered a glass of Guinness, a delightful discovery from a previous visit to the establishment.

"You don't see many a man drinking a pint of that down here." A well-dressed lady, likely in her mid-to-late fifties, addressed him from a few stools down. She raised her glass of the same in toast.

"A lady with class, at last!" Stewart proclaimed as he raised his glass back at her.

She got up from her seat and moved over to clank glasses, then sat down beside him.

"Martha," she said, extending her hand to shake.

"Stewart," he returned. "But shaking hands is for gentlemen," and he leaned over and gave her a polite hug.

"Nice to make your acquaintance, Stewart. Where are you from, back home?"

"Oh, here and there. London area mostly."

He knew enough about the country from his few years living there, and a couple visits back, to fool her about his heritage. It helped that his accent was still there and that in his mind he felt British, even if he was strongly rooted in Canada. The common bond of country got Martha to trust him quicker than she would a complete stranger. After many rounds and accompanying stories, Stewart found himself back at the resort he had abandoned. She wasn't overly attractive, but as he found out during conversation, her bottom line made up for it.

After a couple of days of sightseeing, dining, drinking, and lots of sex, Stewart collected his things from his downtrodden hotel and moved into her suite. Her divorce money was more than she could possibly spend herself and she was quite willing to share her money and her time with her new companion.

"I'm thinking of moving on to the Bahamas, Stewart."

"Oh?" Stewart replied, not sure where she was going with the thought.

"Do you like gambling, love?"

"I've done exceedingly well in my inner circles, and in a few larger games. Nothing big though, only thousand dollar-a-hand stuff." Stewart was not a card shark by any stretch of his imagination, but he knew enough of the games to take some good coin from his Rosedale buddies in the past. That was similar to shooting fish in a barrel, but she didn't need to know that. He was trying to be modest, yet boastful at the same time. It seemed to work.

"Well then, I propose you come with me to the Bahamas to gamble."

"I'm afraid that I don't have the bankroll right now for any big stakes games."

"Not to worry. I'll front you the money," Martha proposed.

"And what kind of a gentleman would I be, taking your money?" Stewart desperately wanted to go, but didn't want to appear to be taking advantage.

"Oh please, Stewart, honey. Think of it as a business venture. We'll split the winnings fifty-fifty." A pleading tone entered her voice.

"I'm still not sure that it is proper."

"Oh, screw proper. We British are far too proper on far too many occasions. Do it for me, please?" While still pleading, there was now a certain sexy pouting going on that was turning Stewart on.

"I suppose, since you insist."

"I'm so excited. You're going to knock them dead; I'm sure of it."

The reconciliation or forgiveness call from his mother almost had Stewart forego the trip to the Bahamas. He wasn't doing anything illegal though, and he didn't want to disappoint his companion after she twisted his arm such and went to all the trouble of booking a presidential suite at the resort. Only a cad would bail on a lady.

Much to his surprise, the cards actually came his way at the tables. After two days of poker, with a few hours of black jack thrown in for fun, Stewart had cleared $100,000. He found it much easier to make decisions when it wasn't his own money on the line. His lady friend gladly gave him half as promised. She wanted Stewart to keep playing, but he knew he had experienced a run of luck the likes of which he would possibly never see again in his life.

At dinner that second night, Martha was excited about their success.

"So, how much do you think you can win by the end of the week?"

"Not so fast, darling. I think my time at the tables is done. It's time to relax and enjoy this magnificent resort!"

"You can't be serious about quitting! You are on such a roll."

"Exactly the time to quit, my dear."

"But , , , "

"No buts about it; it's time to take the money and run." Stewart knew his luck couldn't hold out forever and didn't want to be one of those saps that lose it all back. He was also afraid that she would expect him to continue playing with his half of the money. His nerves would surely get to him if his own money was on the line. And where's the fun in that?

Martha let the topic die at dinner, but brought it up again after some truly gratifying (for both of them) sex.

Stewart seized the opportunity.

"I am utterly offended that you are using me for my card-playing prowess."

"That's not the only prowess I treasure, dear."

"So, you're using me for sex too! I really thought we had something meaningful, possibly even spiritual going on here." Stewart didn't believe anything he was saying, and was quite grateful to be used for sex; after all, her years of experience made for some incredible sessions. But he was also sensing this was his chance to get out clean and head home.

"I didn't mean to offend you, Stewie . . . "

Stewie? That was an abomination. He could put up with a lot, but that would never do.

He didn't say anything, but she could tell he was smouldering.

"Here," and she pulled another stack of money from the safe in the suite. "Take another $25,000 of the winnings. You earned it after all. Now please, please stay."

'Prostitution' he declared, stuffing the money and his belongings into his luggage. "I went from feeling used to feeling bought. If I didn't feel the need to immediately extract myself from your sight, I would bathe to get this feeling off my body." With that, Stewart stormed out of the room and caught the first flight back to the Big Smoke, seed money in hand for his next venture.

Stewart Windle was surprised to find himself back in Toronto so soon. He assumed his self-imposed exile to the Caribbean would be much longer. Not that he particularly enjoyed the blasted heat down there, but it was better than the heat he was facing in Riverdale when he left. Feeling reprieved, Stewart was ready to start over.

9 *The Old Apartment*

Once again Katrina found herself riding the bus. This time she was smiling. It was good to see Cathy, and it was good to see her so happy. Cathy was cautiously excited about her new relationship the last time they met, and it looked like it was still working out. Katrina was a bit disappointed that Cathy had gotten involved again in one of Stewart Windle's ventures, in spite of the last one somehow working out in her favour. There was some aura of dishonesty around Stewart that made Katrina uncomfortable when she thought of him. But she supposed it was an acting gig, as Cathy liked to think of it, and it was better than those depressing lesbian plays that Cathy had toiled in with her psycho, butch roommate.

Katrina forgot to ask Cathy to bring her boyfriend out for drinks tomorrow, but she figured it was probably because she was having troubles with her own relationship. What *was* Jonathan up to? She just knew that he was hiding something.

Katrina intended to go to the salon to close up before heading home, however after cutting the hair of a deceased person, she really felt the need for a shower, a really hot shower that might burn off a layer or two of skin. Fortunately, Kevin had set up the salon's phone number in her cell phone, so she was able to call him without too much trouble and get him to close up.

Fortunately, the sun had broken through and the winds were in the single digits. The walk from the bus stop to her apartment wouldn't feel so cold today. As she approached their apartment, Jonathan's car wasn't anywhere to be seen in the regular parking spaces on the road. She headed up the stairs to their third floor unit, stopping to grab the usual junk mail on the way up. As she walked in the door, his cat Morris came to greet her, likely wanting food. Who is so lame to name a cat Morris? That should have been a sign, she thought.

She didn't like to jump in the shower right away after coming in from the cold. Her mother had told her a story about her Aunt Edith passing out in the shower one day after coming in from the cold and jumping right into a hot shower. What her mother didn't tell her was that Aunt Edith had quite a drinking problem, and had only gone into the shower in a futile attempt to sober up. Her aunt was *really* drunk though, so she went into the shower fully dressed — winter boots, parka, scarf, toque, and gloves. They weren't sure if the heat from the scalding water and three layers of clothes caused her to pass out, or if she was simply so wasted that she would have passed out wherever she happened to be at the time. Aunt Edith was likely lucky that she didn't pass out in some snow bank between farms near Pipton. She wouldn't have been found until spring thaw. Regardless of the reason, it made a great story that all of the parents in Pipton used to ensure their kid's body temperatures settled before jumping in the tub or shower.

Heeding the childhood warning, Katrina came in and removed her winter layer and hung them in the tiny closet by the door. She decided to go into the kitchen and feed the cat. She popped open a cold beer and sat to thaw herself out for a few minutes. She didn't realize it, but she was guzzling her beer down while thinking about Jonathan. The anxiety was making her drink much quicker than normal. She finished her beer in about five minutes; about twenty-five minutes quicker than her normal nursing, as Jonathan called it. She figured she had thawed long enough and went to hop in the shower.

Their bathroom certainly wouldn't make any house magazines, although it was perfectly suited for 'Trash this Place,' a home flipping show. The toilet didn't leak. That was the only positive thing she could think about the room. The door wouldn't stay closed, which was not so great for hosting parties. The tiles on the walls and floors were a faded 1950's yellow, with bits of corners broken off in many places. The tub didn't look clean, no matter how hard she scrubbed it or how long she left the 'Majic Scrub' soak in. She figured that at some time the grout was white, but it had turned very dark now. But worst of all was the water pressure. They had talked to the landlord endlessly about getting better water pressure, and he always came up with some lame excuse. She was tired of trying to get shampoo out of her hair for ten minutes each time she showered. By then, of course, the water had turned cold.

Katrina summoned her courage and stepped into the tub. She couldn't turn the water on ahead of time for fear of losing some portion of the two minutes of hot water that she was going to get. She crossed her one arm in front of her breasts and bent down to turn on the water. Shit, she thought, that was cold. She started immediately shampooing her hair. Sure enough, the bathroom door popped slightly open and a cold draft found its way into the shower, hitting her on the back. Just at that moment, she heard Jonathan come in the door. She was about to yell his name, but because of the pathetic water pressure and the door popping open, she could hear him talking. Must be on the phone, she thought.

Jonathon came into the apartment with his cell phone glued to his ear.

"Hold on a sec," as he switched hands to put his bag down and pull out a folded page of the sports section.

"Okay. I need you to put $500 on the Leafs tonight, taking the goal and a half spread. Yeah, I'm good for it. I don't care what you heard about me losing money at Casinorama. I'm good for the $500. Look. Tomorrow's the day I'm supposed to do the bank deposit, so I'll just skim the $500 off the top. No biggie. Besides, I got a feeling about tonight. The Leafs are going to break out of their slump, and the Wings winning streak has got to end sometime, right? Good. I'll see you at Johnny's tomorrow to collect."

Jonathan knew that he was seriously close to getting in too deep with the gambling. He'd managed to keep reasonably even the previous few years, with a few high spots here and there. This year, though, had been a bad one. He was definitely on a cold streak, much like his Leafs.

He couldn't recall such a cold streak since his second year at the university. He told his mother that he'd just lost the appetite for business school part way through the term, but the real reason was that he had to use the tuition money to pay off his debts to bookies threatening to hurt him. He actually hadn't even started his second year, except to hang around campus for a couple of weeks as a cover for saying why he couldn't get the tuition money back from the university.

But this time he knew it was different. It was only a matter of time until he hit that one big score that would get him out of debt and set him up for a while. He had given up on the lotteries, believing them to be nothing but luck and a fool's game. He intended to use his knowledge of sports, and his natural good luck, to hit the big one. He imagined quitting his job at his sister's place, and taking Katrina on a month-long trip to the Caribbean . . . nothing but Corona and Katrina. A Leaf's upset win tonight would act as a good start. He decided that he better head to his lucky bar to watch the game.

The next thing Katrina heard was the door closing and Jonathan thumping down the stairs to go outside. She was stunned. She knew something was up, but she didn't think that Jonathan would ever steal from her. Katrina wondered how long this had been going on, and how much he had skimmed. Maybe that's what Debbie meant when she made a smart remark about Jonathan never visiting with her. He was likely at the casino most of the time he went up there.

Katrina was really ticked off. And then the water went cold, to boot. She got out of the shower and toweled off. She headed into the living room to call Jonathan's cell from the house phone, as Kevin hadn't programmed Jonathan's number in yet. Kevin kept avoiding her whenever she asked. Katrina dialed the number and listened to it ring, and ring. Then, the voice mail kicked in. Prick, she thought. She had seen his phone enough to know that the house number would come up with her name on the display since the bill was in her name. So he purposely wasn't answering it. At least he was likely gone for the night so they wouldn't play the game where she would try to start conversation and he would avoid it or ignore her. They had played that game the last few nights and it was wearing thin on her. At least she'd get the bed to herself tonight, knowing that he'd sneak in late and crash on the couch.

10   *Waking on the Couch*

Daylight came to their apartment, piercing through the makeshift arrangement of blankets that Jonathan called curtains. He woke up sprawled on the couch. Jonathan moved his head so that he could look at his watch without moving too much.

Eight thirty A.M. He closed his eyes and he thought. Katrina was already gone to catch her bus, so he wouldn't have to avoid her this morning, or worry about an argument starting his day off on the wrong foot. He was probably going to get an earful from his sister anyway, as there was no way he was going to get to her modeling agency by 9:00 A.M. So he'd arrive late again. Big friggin' deal. Besides, he usually put in ten-hour days for eight hours of pay. She should have more understanding. She's always there on time to open up, so it's not like he's keeping people waiting in the cold by him arriving late.

Jonathan slowly opened his eyes. First one eye opened, then after thinking about it, the other one cracked open. It was one of those really bright winter mornings, where a fresh layer of snow was magnifying the sun's brightness into an almost blinding glare. It was too bright for him on this morning, considering the number of beers that he consumed last night. Out of nervousness he always drank more when the game was close. That coupled with a deal on Upper Canada Ale, and he had managed to give himself a bit of a hangover this morning.

He decided the best course of action was to close his eyes again for a few more minutes. Hell, what's the difference between 30 and 45 minutes late? Besides, Jonathan wasn't in a really good mood. His Leaf's had the Wings tied at two, with only three minutes left to play. It looked like a lock when the Leafs got a two-man power play. After all, he was holding a spread of a goal and a half. But the Leafs gave up a short- handed goal on the five on three, then another one with their net empty while trying to get the equalizer. Poof! Just like that, the game was blown 4-2. Spread two. Five hundred dollars gone.

In spite of all of these thoughts, he decided it was finally time to open his eyes and keep them open for the day. He slowly sat up on the couch, but hesitated when he heard the sound of paper crinkling. He saw a couple of sticky notes fall to the ground. As he bent down to pick them up, he noticed that he had about twenty more stuck to his shirt and pants. He plucked one off his chest. "Asshole" was all it said. He looked at another. "Asshole," again, and again. He picked the rest of them off his body without reading them. He grabbed one off of the floor. "Big Asshole" — well that one was more creative.

Jonathan got up from the couch and as he walked by the cat on the way to the bathroom, he stuck a couple of the notes on it. Morris looked up at him and let out a snarl that sounded in a strange way like the word "Asshole."

He needed a cold shower today to get him going. This, of course, was no problem since the hot water only worked for a few minutes at a time. The landlord said it was going to cost him over two grand to replace the pipes to improve the water pressure and to get a new hot water heater. Since it would come out of the landlord's pocket, he offered Jonathan a deal. The landlord offered him $50 off their rent each month if they would just live with the problems. Jonathan took the deal, but never told Katrina about it. He didn't split the rent savings with her either, as then he'd have to tell her about the deal. And he knew that she'd take the hot water getting fixed instead of the $50 a month.

Having finished getting ready for work, Jonathan headed down the stairs out of the apartment building. He glanced at his watch again, 9:30 A.M. While he knew it would add a few minutes to his tardiness, he decided he better swing by Tim Horton's and pick up a double, double large coffee for his sister. Jonathan figured he better get her a chocolate chip muffin too, just in case she was in a bad mood even before she found out he was late again.

As he went to pull into the parking lot at the agency, he cursed at the flower truck blocking the entrance. It was trying to pull out, but was dead centre in the middle of the opening. It was a good thing that Jonathan got the muffin, as he usually handled all the deliveries, and his sister would be pissed now for sure having to do his job. The truck made him wait only a minute or so, but since he was already late, it felt much longer. As the florist's truck started to edge out into traffic, it came to Jonathan that the flower delivery was actually a good thing. He had a dinner date with Katrina tonight, and apparently she thought he was acting like a jerk toward her lately. Alright, between the cottage episode and last night, he had been an asshole. So flowers were definitely in order for tonight, and now he wouldn't have to pay for them. He'd just have to scoop a bunch up before his sister sent them all to the senior's home at the end of the day. She always did so after using flowers for a photo shoot.

11   *Owen*

It was mid-afternoon and the salon had steady clientele all day. A slightly above average day, but nothing worth writing home about. And Katrina still wrote home. She was the only person in her generation that she knew to still write letters, not that she didn't appreciate the immediacy of a phone call and the joy of hearing her parents' voices over the phone. She just really enjoyed sitting down with a cup of coffee on a Sunday afternoon and writing a heartfelt letter. She could express herself more freely and without feeling time-boxed into a worry-about-the-cost long distance call. Katrina didn't understand most of the functions of her new cell phone, and had little to no capability of understanding the convoluted cell phone plan she had hastily chosen.

Katrina was finishing sweeping up from a recently departed customer, something that Jonathan told her to get Kevin or Marlene to do. After all, she was the boss and shouldn't have to stoop to such labour. Katrina actually enjoyed sweeping, and was often chided by Kevin for whistling while she did it, as was the case today.

"Hey, Bashful, where are the other dwarfs today?" he poked fun at her.

"Funny. I guess that would make you Gay-ly," she returned. She took a couple of more sweeps, and then bent down, dust pan in one hand, broom in the other, to collect the trimmings and bag them. As she was kneeling on the floor, the bell over the door rang, and another sharply dressed man entered. Katrina immediately thought of the lawyer from the other day. God help her if another one of her clientele had passed away.

Sensing Katrina's nervousness, Marlene approached the visitor. "Can I help you?" All the while Marlene was checking out the cut of the man's suit. He was an impressive figure for Marlene to leer at. She was pretty good at sizing men up. In her mind she calculated – about 6 foot 3, likely about 230 pounds, size 12 feet, and large hands. This guy had potential, she thought. That frame and the size of those appendages were likely a sign of another prominent feature that she wouldn't mind investigating.

"Is Katrina, the owner of this salon, present at this time?" the man asked.

"Of course, again . . . " sighed Marlene.

"Yes, over here," Katrina replied, just getting up from her crouch.

"I have a private matter to discuss with you. Is there someplace we can talk?"

"What's this about? There is really no private place. The backroom doesn't have a door, and it's kind of cluttered."

"The bathroom has a door," Kevin chirped in.

"That's okay. We can just talk here, Mr. ???"

"Owen. Bill Owen," he replied. "From Ketchum Owen Collection Agency."

Katrina looked over at Kevin. Was this guy for real? She'd heard that a lot of people gravitate to professions that come from their names, but this sounded too corny to be real. She gave Kevin a stare, thinking this was his doing. And Kevin would certainly have reason to pull some kind of stunt. It wasn't too long ago, about a week before Kevin's birthday, that Katrina had herself pulled a stunt on him. She had hired a couple of male strippers to pose as police officers and come in to arrest Kevin. They stood him up against the wall and frisked him, accusing him of playing a mule on his trip back from Mexico, telling him they were going to have to perform a complete cavity search. They even went so far as to handcuff him to one of the stylist chairs. Ron was in on it and watching from the backroom, but his jealousy got the best of him and he couldn't take it anymore. Katrina wasn't sure whether Kevin was humiliated or thrilled by the experience. She thought that Kevin acted humiliated for Ron's sake, and that deep down it was one of the best birthday presents ever. So, Katrina waited for just this moment for weeks. With the build on this guy, he had to have come from one of the strip clubs. Katrina was convinced it was a gag and jumped right into this prank.

"Bill Owen, eh? Have I been naughty Bill?" and she moved up close to him, sliding her hand up his tie. "What punishment have you got in mind for me? Do you like to Ketchum with their pants down Bill? Perhaps a little spanking?"

Kevin and Marlene both stood with their mouths agape.

Bill wasn't sure what to do. He started to turn red. Then he started to stammer.

"I uh, don't uh, know uh, what you mean. I'm here due to your debts."

"Oh, I see. I have to pay my debt to society for being a bad girl," as she ran her fingers slowly up his shoulder and around his ear. Her other hand started down the inside of his shirt toward his belt.

At this point, Bill couldn't take it anymore. He stepped firmly back, knocking over one of the chairs along the wall before coming to a stop a few paces away from the vixen. He stood up straight, and adjusted his tie to regain his composure.

"I'm here to serve you official notice about your past due bills," he shouted in quick fashion, making sure he got the words out before she could accost him again.

Katrina looked at Kevin. "You mean you didn't put him up to this?" Her face began to change colour to a bright red shade of embarrassment.

Kevin lifted his shoulders and said "Sorry dear, not my doing."

"Me neither," followed Marlene, just as Katrina's focus shifted to her.

Trying to regain her composure, Katrina turned back to Bill Owen.

"What do you mean official notice?"

"The salon rent hasn't been paid for four months, and neither has your hydro. The loan to fix this place up hasn't been paid in that time either."

"What loan? We had enough to fix it up with the cash I had, with money left in the bank!"

"Sorry Miss, but we've sent notices in the mail the last two months with no reply. So a personal visit happens in these situations. You need to come up with $10,000 by a week from Friday or I'll be forced to close this place and seize its assets."

Katrina just stood there stunned. Her beautiful complexion had faded and was supplanted with a pale skin tone. She looked like she was going to faint. And she did.

When Katrina awoke, she was sitting propped up in one of the stylist chairs. Marlene's arm was around her to ensure she wasn't going to slide out of the chair and onto the floor. Kevin leaned over in front of her, trying to get her to drink some water. She was trying to figure out how she got here.

"Stripper . . . no bill collector . . . " as she tried to remember.

"Take it easy, Kat," Marlene tried to reassure her. "Take a few deep breaths."

"She's not pregnant, you ditz." Kevin scolded Marlene.

"Broke . . . I'm broke!" Katrina blurted out, followed by "I'm going to kill him."

"He's gone Kat. The bill collector's gone."

"Not him. Jonathon. I gave Jonathan the money to setup the place and he's managed the bills since we started. He told me to focus on building the clientele and keeping them happy. You know, concentrate on what I do best and not worry about the hassles of the money side. He even made all the bank deposits — at least I thought he did. I never even checked. I just overheard him last night talking to someone about skimming money, but I didn't think he'd been doing it all along. Jonathan's the one with the business degree. I trusted him."

"Technically, he only finished one year of business school," Kevin said in a somewhat cautious voice.

"Technically, I'm going to kill him," and she got up from their guardianship. She went over to the phone and dialed. No answer at home. No answer on the cell. She was supposed to meet him for dinner at La Belle Cuisine tonight. It would have to wait until then. By then she'd be ready to cook him.

12 *The Wake*

Katrina returned to the funeral home. This time her visit was for Duncan's service. She wondered how to say goodbye to someone she barely knew anything about. Why should her heart feel so sad for this man? Duncan was a regular customer, but it's not like they talked extensively or anything. Usually they exchanged a few polite lines like 'Crazy weather, eh?' Duncan wasn't rude; he just wasn't a talker.

Katrina entered the funeral home and acknowledged Granderson's presence with a smile and polite nod. She went straight to the coatroom and shed her winter coverings, carefully stuffing her scarf and toque into the right arm of her coat. Her mother taught her that little trick. And it had to be the right arm since it went in first . . . you didn't want to have the right arm of your coat on and have to fumble with a left arm full of scarf and toque.

Back into the foyer she stepped, looking around until she spotted the room for Duncan's service. Katrina was surprised to walk into a room full of lively chatter and people. She wondered how a seemingly homeless guy would know so many people. Then she spotted

Cathy and knew there were FREDs present. But how could Duncan afford to rent funeral guests?

"Hello, Miss! Tammy Morgan. I knew Duncan from MIT." Cathy had easily shifted into a new role for today's job. Cathy gave Katrina a wink and a smile.

"Oh, yes. I'm Katrina, Duncan's stylist. Pleased to meet you," and she extended her hand out for a polite shake.

"Excuse me, folks," came a voice over the microphone from the front of the room. It was the funeral director Ben Better's voice. "Could you all kindly take your seats, please?" After a few moments of rustling around, everyone found a chair. Katrina sat next to Cathy, or should she say Tammy.

"This afternoon's service will consist of three parts. The first part will be a service by our good friend Reverend O'Reilly. Following his sermon, at the request of Mr. McAllister's family, we will ask that friends of the late Mr. McAllister come to the podium and share some of their memories with all of us as a way of rejoicing in his life. And for the last part, we will close the doors and have a good old fashioned Irish wake."

As the Catholic priest did his bit to prepare Duncan's soul for the 'journey to our Lord's kingdom', Katrina thought about what she could say. 'He was a nice guy; I liked him' was lame and uninteresting. She decided it was best to leave any storytelling to people who knew him better than she did.

"Now let us all bow our heads in prayer . . ." The reverend closed in on his finale. Katrina realized that she hadn't even gone up to see the body before the service started. She stood up slightly in her chair, but couldn't see much and almost had the chair fold up on her from behind. She carefully sat back down and bent her head down for one final 'Amen'.

"Thank you, Reverend O'Reilly. Uplifting words we should all remember." Ben Better had taken the podium again. "So do we have any immediate family members that would like to say anything?" A man in his late fifties sat alone in the front row on the one side. It was likely Duncan's father, Katrina supposed. She could see only part of his profile, but saw enough to see a resemblance. The poor man simply shook his head and uncomfortably shifted his legs where he sat.

A man a few rows back slowly stood up and moved to the front. He stopped for a second to look at Duncan, and then moved in front of the microphone.

"For those that don't know me, I'm Fred Golding."

Great, thought Katrina. All these FREDs here, and we have a real Fred. Well, maybe a real Fred. She wasn't sure if this was a FRED calling himself Fred.

"I worked with Duncan for the last five years, since he returned from university. He was obviously a very bright man, who fought and overcame illness in his youth to still lead a productive life. In his few years in the industry, he researched and developed five patents that will likely generate millions in profits for his father's company in years to come. We can only imagine the potential of his life if it hadn't been tragically cut short. But let's not dwell on the sad. Instead, let's think of all the good those patents will do to improve the lives of others. Thank you." The gentleman looked up slightly at the crowd and then stepped away from the front.

Katrina was still soaking in some of the new revelations about this mystery man named Duncan. She now knew he was a genius and his father was apparently rich. So why would Duncan dress like he did and act the loner part?

At that moment, Cathy got up from her seat and headed toward the speaker's mark. As she got to the front, she made a few minor wardrobe adjustments that were planned to draw attention to 'all the right stuff', as she once referred to it to Katrina.

"My name is Tammy Morgan. Most of you don't know me. I got to know Duncan while he was at MIT. I was attending a, well, let's just say a slightly less prestigious college in Boston. We met at a coffee shop that students from both schools frequented. Many of the girls from my school went there to try and land a brainy nerd like Duncan for a husband. You know the quiet type that had never . . . I mean that weren't overly graceful around women. The girls saw these guys as walking money belts, and were sure they could fix the guy's social deficiencies or at least settle for a few million at divorce time.

So I tell you, when I first met Duncan, I thought he fit the mold. I wasn't there on a mission like many of my school sisters. Likely if I had been, he would have ignored me altogether. I was there pumping down caffeine while prepping for an exam. Somehow we got to talking, and the next thing I knew, he was telling me his 'exam theory'. He told me how there were different types of exams, and that he believed he knew the most effective study method for each type. The analytical mind that Duncan possessed was amazing." She looked down at Duncan's father. "I got an 82 on my exam the next day, applying Duncan's theory. It was the first time that I had broken 70 in three terms, and I felt like I studied less.

We became friends over the next year or so, often meeting for coffee. Stupid me though, I didn't know enough to dump that jerk I was dating at the time. All these geniuses around and I'm stuck on some loser musician-wannabe with no goals in life except getting stoned after a good gig. Anyway, Duncan told me that I had helped him to relax when the pressure of his schedule was getting to him. I guess it's tough when you're only number two in your class at MIT!"

The gathering laughed at a few of her remarks, releasing some of the built up tension of the situation.

"Well, I know when to quit. Thanks everyone for listening," and Cathy returned to her seat, acknowledging some smiles and nods on the way back.

"That was awesome, Cathy!" Katrina whispered excitedly to her.

"Thanks. Pretty good improvising from this card, eh?" and she handed Kat a card that simply said:

> "Tammy Morgan. Friend from Boston. Duncan second in class at MIT."

Another person had already begun speaking and had people laughing out loud at a couple of his anecdotes.

"This guy's good too," Cathy bumped Katrina's arm to get her attention. "I've heard him at a couple of other gigs. I think he's part time at the Krazy Komedy House."

"He's a FRED, too?!"

"You bet. Funny as hell. Too bad he's nothing to look at. Not that I'm looking anyway," Cathy added quickly to cut off any remark from Katrina. As the comic FRED finished, Ben came back to the front, wanting to end the personal comments portion of the service on a high note.

"Ladies and gentlemen, we now will take a short break to allow anyone under nineteen to be accompanied out of this room, so that we may start the wake portion of the service. Beer, wine, and mixed drinks come compliments of Duncan's father, as do the many finger foods at the back." Everyone turned to see the bountiful spread that covered the tables. Katrina hadn't seen anything like this at a funeral before.

"C'mon Kat, let's go get a drink. I think I've earned one!" as Cathy practically dragged Katrina out of her seat. As they walked away from the bar with their red wines in hand, Katrina asked Cathy to view the body with her. "My least favourite part, to tell you the truth. I don't mind talking about the dead, but I can't stand looking at them. Sounds cold, but they never look the same. Not that I knew what he looked like, but without seeing the eyes it just doesn't seem right.

"I know what you mean. My folks always made me go up, saying you need to see someone like that to really, truly accept that they are gone."

"That's probably true, but I'd rather remember them smiling and laughing than lying there like that."

The two ladies approached the casket, neither appearing really sure they wanted to be there. Katrina just noticed that they were playing music, and smiled hearing the words from an old song by The Odds that she particularly liked. 'Carrying your ashes from bar to bar' the song started. The song was about a guy carrying a friend's ashes to all their favourite watering holes as his way of saying goodbye.

"Hey, he doesn't look half bad! And his hair looks great Kat. Nice job!" a surprised Cathy told Katrina.

"Thanks, Cathy."

"It makes you wonder though," Cathy started, "why they put this guy in a $600 suit, then throw a knock-off watch on him."

"What do you mean? He's got a GUCCI. I saw it yesterday," Katrina replied, leaning forward to look into the casket.

"No. It's a QUCCI, see?" and Cathy slightly lifted his wrist to show it. "Let me check out the pocket watch."

Before Katrina could say no, Cathy already had it in her hand, flipping it over a couple of times.

"Yup, cheap imitation. Not even gold plated."

"It can't be! It was an antique yesterday. It must have been a couple hundred years old."

"Well, maybe the family wanted to keep the good stuff as keepsakes."

"Maybe. Now let me put that back," and as Katrina reached for the pocket watch, she knocked it out of Cathy's hand and into the casket.

"Shit, Kat! I can't see where it went."

"Sorry. I'll reach down at his side. It must have slid down there." As Katrina leaned further over the side of the casket, she forgot that she had a drink in the other hand. She brought her other hand forward to hold the side of the casket for balance, and dumped the remaining red wine all over Duncan's suit and white shirt!

They looked at each other in disbelief.

"What do we do now?" asked Katrina.

"What do you mean, 'we'?" a defensive Cathy replied.

"You've got to help me. I don't know what to do!" a frantic Katrina grabbed at Cathy's arm. This, of course, caused Cathy to spill her red wine too, also dumping its contents into the casket.

"At least mine just hit his pants," chuckled Cathy. "Nobody would know unless they bent over to smell him."

"Let's close the lid," blurted out Katrina, pleased with her sudden inspiration.

"Don't you think someone will notice?"

"No. No. They'll assume the caretakers did it. Help me close it and put some flowers on top."

"You're crazy, you know that? I think you're finally catching on to some of my tricks. Maybe you're finally shedding that shy girl persona."

"Desperate times, I guess. Are you going to help?"

"Help with what?" came the voice of Ben Better from behind the two ladies. He walked up between the two of them and saw the extent of the mess they had caused. "Oh, I see. Well, this is a new one. I guess it could have been worse," he said, trying to cheer up Katrina.

"How?" she wondered aloud.

"Well, it could have been vomit. But then I've seen that before."

"That's gross," the ladies said in unison.

"You get used to it, amongst other things," Ben shrugged. "You girls just mosey to the back and get some food. I'll close him up and fix it later."

As they walked to the back, they saw Ben close the casket and gently place a vase of flowers on top.

"See, I told you it was a good idea," whispered Katrina.

"Lucky guess," Cathy answered back. "More wine?"

. . . and the song finished about spilling his friends' ashes on the floor of the bar and . . . . 'I'll laugh as people slip on you coming in this door . . . '

Dale J. Moore

13 *Dinner, Out*

As Katrina put on her coat at the funeral home, she was feeling a slight buzz from the couple of glasses of wine. It really was likely less than one small glass, having spilled most of her first glass on Duncan and having only sipped on the second glass before leaving it somewhere. Of course, it didn't take much for her to get a buzz. She wrapped her new scarf around the back of her neck and neatly tucked it in the front collar of her coat. Katrina started to pull her toque over her blonde hair when she suddenly remembered her dinner date with Jonathan tonight.

She decided that she did not have time to go back to the apartment to change, so she hopped on a different bus that would take her to La Belle Cuisine. She wanted to talk to Ben about the changed jewelry on Duncan, but didn't have a chance. She figured it could wait until tomorrow. Hopefully, Ben wouldn't think that it was strange of her to ask, but she really needed to know. It sounded like Ben had seen his fair share of strange over the years, so her little question probably wouldn't even cause him to blink.

The bus pulled up to her stop. The restaurant was about half way between this stop and the next, so she decided to get off at the first one and walk. It wasn't until after she got off the bus that she found out that getting off at the first stop meant walking into the bitter wind to the restaurant, instead of having it at her back if she had gotten off at the next one. She reached the front door not much worse for wear in spite of the cold. The cold was much worse in the country than the city due to the heat generated by the city. The buildings tended to block some of the wind, but she was still caught off guard sometimes by the wind tunnels that existed in Toronto. Her toque had kept her hair from becoming a scary mess.

"Good evening, Miss," came the greeting from the maitre d', although he didn't seem overly thrilled about his job. Katrina didn't care for the all-too-authentic French attitudes at La Belle Cuisine. She certainly liked the French-Canadian hospitality she had experienced in Montreal much better than this pretentious 'I'm a real French restaurant' thing they had going on here. "Monsieur Jonathan's usual table is ready. Please follow me."

Katrina hated all the airs that people put on at this place. It wasn't her style at all, having come from a small town, but Jonathan seemed to soak it up. It was odd though, as he didn't seem like the type when they first met. It seemed like only the last month or two that he started with the rich guy persona. Maybe it was from hanging around models all day at his sister's studio. Maybe he felt the need to impress people. She started to feel self-conscious that all he really was using her for was some sort of trophy girlfriend.

She sat down and looked around. When it was first built a long time ago, the place was likely a couple of small stores with living quarters up above. At some point, an owner gutted the building and knocked the walls out to make a fairly sizeable establishment. It looked even larger with the upstairs now gone, giving it very high ceilings. Katrina liked the solid wood that permeated the place as it almost made up for the wooden wait staff.

"Can I get Mademoiselle a nice merlot tonight?" as he handed her the wine list.

"No, but thank-you. I'll wait for Jonathan."

"Can I get you a bottle of Monsieur Jonathan's usual?"

"I suppose that would be fine," she replied, mostly to get rid of him.

"May I?" the waiter asked as he reached over to take the wine menu from her.

"No, it's okay, I want to look at it some more," and she pulled it close to her body. What she really wanted was to see how much Jonathan was dropping on a bottle of 'the usual'. The waiter soon reappeared with the bottle and a couple of glasses. He slit the top wrapper and undressed the top, exposing the cork. He then removed the cork seemingly with almost no effort. She wasn't a big fan of wine and the effort to open a bottle seem unjustifiable to her. Her palate couldn't really tell the difference between the good stuff and a bottle of wine with a twist off cap (or from a box of wine for that matter). The waiter poured the smallest amount into her glass and handed it to her, at the same time presenting the cork for her to appreciate. Katrina ignored the cork, and grabbing her glass, gulped down the half-ounce or so that he had poured.

"Fine" was her simple reply. The waiter gave her a rude look, like it was a waste to serve her anything more than swill from a bucket. As he walked away, Katrina twirled the bottle around to see the label. She then plucked the wine list from the table and started flipping through it. Her finger ran up and down the pages, searching for the brand selected by Jonathan. Finally, there it was, $172 a bottle.

"Shit!" she accidently said out loud, and loud enough to be heard by the couple that sat an empty table away from her. "Sorry."

How the hell does he afford this? She started doing some math in her head, which was truly uncommon for Katrina. Let's see. Jonathan usually comes here twice a week, once with her, and once or twice a week with clients. Multiply that times four weeks a month. That's about ten to twelve bottles a month at $172 each. That's about . . . she wasn't sure, but she figured somewhere between $1,500 and $2,000 a month just on wine. Not to mention the price of dinner and tipping the snooty French waiters. She knew his job at his sisters didn't pay that well. She was starting to get angry. How the hell does he afford this? She had an uneasy feeling that she knew where the money had come from.

Before she could cool down, she overheard someone around the corner at the front door. "Monsieur Jonathan, so good to see you, sir. Your lovely guest is already seated at your table."

"Merci, Marcel. Good to see you too!" and around the corner he came. Jonathan absolutely looked the part tonight. He was in a sharp suit, French cuff of course, with an expensive shirt and tie that Katrina had bought him for Christmas. She had spent more on that shirt and tie than all the other presents she bought for her entire family. She had felt really guilty about it at the time, but he did look like a million bucks in it. He had the appearance of a model in that outfit.

Jonathan knew he was likely going to spend most of the night making up to Katrina. He was prepared to beg forgiveness. He also knew from previous experience that his favourite wine went straight to Katrina's head and mellowed her out. Coupled with the fresh flowers, he should be off the hook.

"Hey, hon. I see Francois brought you my wine!" He smiled, flashed the flowers in front of her, and leaned over to kiss her on the cheek. Unfortunately, it was the wrong way to start the conversation, mentioning the wine that is.

"Yes. I saw the price on it too!" she threw back at him, the seat of his suit barely having hit his chair. "How can you afford this?" she followed.

"Hey, hey. Good to see you too! And don't I deserve to spoil myself after a hard day at work? It's not like I drink this stuff every day."

"No, but almost every second day."

"I work hard you know. You don't know the stress I'm under at work."

"Yeah, it must be tough with all those super-model types smothering you all day. Having to see them almost naked everyday could stress out any guy."

"Can we change the conversation please?" as Jonathan ignored eye contact and glanced over his menu, as if he even needed to look at it.

"Sure. Let's talk about a visit I got today . . . "

At that moment, Francois appeared to leave some warm bread and take their order.

"Miss, have you decided?"

"Oh yes. I'll have the Poolette rot eye."

"Does miss mean the *Poulet Roti*?"

"Yes, whatever."

"*Et Monsieur?*"

"*Le Coquille St. Jacques*, s'il vous plait."

"*Tres bien, monsieur*" and Francois closed up his ordering book and sharply turned to make his way toward the kitchen.

"He's a snob and doesn't like me," Katrina whispered.

"He's French. He doesn't like most people," replied Jonathon, as he buttered a steamy section of bread for Katrina, then one for himself.

"Anyway, I was starting about my visit from Bill Owen."

"Who?"

"He's a bill collector."

Jonathan coughed, apparently partially gagging on the bread he had just started to eat. "A what?"

"You heard me. A bill collector. He says that we haven't paid any bills in months and that I owe $10,000 by next Friday."

Jonathon tried to backpedal his way out of the discussion.

"There must be some mistake. I've paid the bills regularly."

"What about the loan? He says you took a loan out to remodel, and didn't use the cash I gave you."

Again, Jonathan tried to navigate his way out.

"I took out a small loan, because I wanted to use some of your money to put hand railings and a ramp up at my mother's to make it safer for her."

She had seen the railings and ramp. She also knew from talking to his mother that her daughter had bought them and her son-in-law had installed them.

"Why are you lying to me?" Katrina started to raise her voice.

"Keep it down." Jonathan motioned with his hand, looking around to see if anyone was paying attention.

"And I heard you last night on the phone. Are you gambling a lot?"

"If you didn't have all those people working at your salon, you'd make money on your stupid little business. I don't know why I ever agreed to help you out."

Katrina was close to the edge.

"Stupid little business? Helping me out? You've helped me out of all my money by the looks of it. I'm not sure whether I'm more upset with you stealing from me or lying to me. It doesn't matter." She stood up quickly knocking her chair backwards. The chair hit an empty one behind her and then fell in front of a waiter passing by, sending him and the two orders on his arm crashing to the floor at Jonathan's feet. Unfortunately, thought Katrina, it wasn't Francois. Jonathan was incredibly embarrassed and tried to slump in his chair so not many people would see it was his table.

But, Katrina wasn't through.

"I want you out. I won't put up with the lies or the stealing. You can get your stuff tomorrow when I'm at work trying to figure out how to save my stupid little business. And you can take your fancy schmancy French food and shove it . . . well, you know." At that point, Francois had reappeared from the kitchen, unaware of the trouble until he got near the table. He had their food ready to serve. Katrina gave him a menacing look, grabbed her plate from him, and dropped it on the table. She then grabbed the chicken with her bare hand.

"Here. I hope my poolet rotties on your face," and she threw it at Jonathon, striking him partially on the face, but mostly landing squarely on his chest and the expensive shirt and tie she had bought. "Shit," she said "what a waste of a beautiful shirt and tie," and she turned to head out. She then changed her mind and did an about-face. Francois still stood there in a stupor, still holding Jonathan's dish.

"And same to you," she said, and flipped Jonathan's food onto Francois.

She walked a few steps and grabbed for her coat on the wall-mounted hook. It, of course, stuck on the hook, and pulled her backward for a second before she regained her composure and was able to unhook it from its resting place. As she walked by the maitre d' at the door, she looked at him and his nose turned up in the air.

"And o' friggen woir to you too," and she went out the door, feeling proud of herself for dumping Jonathan's sorry ass. She stood in front of La Belle Cuisine and looked around. She looked at her watch. She then realized that she probably couldn't go back in and ask Jonathan for a ride home. She looked at the street again. No sign of a bus. She likely missed the last one. She looked at her cell phone. She didn't have a number for the taxi company. She could go back in and ask the maitre d' to call her a cab — likely not a good idea. So, she decided to suck it up and walk until she could flag down a cab.

Dale J. Moore

14 Roots

Some people exist in Toronto. Marlene loved living there. She loved everything about it. She grew up in Atwood, a small farming town where you knew everybody by name. You even knew most of the people in the next town because you shared the school with them. She enjoyed the comfort that the small town provided her, but she wasn't a farm girl at heart. Actually, her family wasn't farmers at all. Her dad was the town barber and county reeve. Her mom worked part time at the feed store. That was the closest that Marlene got to farming. She knew it was hard labour operating a farm, and quite frankly, she wasn't interested in farming or becoming a farmer's wife and part-time something or other. She sensed the satisfaction and contentment that came from that lifestyle, but she had other aspirations.

Like many young girls, Marlene looked up to her father and she was definitely daddy's little girl. Her mom tried taking Marlene into work a few times in the summer months when she was eight or nine years old. Marlene thought it was neat to poke holes in the feedbags with a pen and watch the contents pour out into little mounds on the floor. She also ran amuck in the store wrapping everything with bailing twine. The owner of the store was not impressed with her games and politely asked her mother not to bring her back. He said it was the last straw, an expression that Marlene didn't understand at the time. She knew that bailing twine was used for straw, but didn't get why it was the last straw.

As a result of her misadventures at the feed store, Marlene spent most of her summer days at the barbershop. And while she occasionally got in trouble for finger painting the barber chairs with Brill Cream or using her dad's scissors to cut her glued together artwork, her dad always got a laugh out of it. Her dad always told her mother of the events at work. He would say that he sat her in the corner for an hour after each episode as a timeout, but he never did.

As Marlene got older, she began to take notice of what her Dad's job entailed. She knew that he was good at it because everyone left with a smile and always came back. The customers could have gone to Listowel to a fancier (and pricier) salon, but they came back. She also realized how much her father enjoyed his job. He loved the personal interactions, even if it meant comforting someone who was grieving as they got a cut before a funeral. He was in his glory telling one of his seemingly endless supply of stories and jokes. He had a knack for taking someone else's account of an event and turning it into a hilarious twenty-minute scene. Marlene would often hear the same story five or ten times during a day, while sweeping up and doing odd chores. Somehow her father had a way of making each version slightly different. She always thought he could have had success as a stand-up comedian if he wanted to leave for the big city. Her dad started to get her involved in the story telling over time, having her act out the roles of the women in his stories.

Her dad made work so much fun that it inspired her to leave for London to take up hairdressing in the fall after graduating. She knew there was no going back to Atwood to live after she finished styling school. And though London was a nice city, she decided to make the big leap and head to Toronto.

Marlene had worked at a few crappy places when she first started working. It took some getting used to the commotion of a large city. She tried talkative and funny at her first job. The owner told her to go down to the Comedy Cradle if she wanted to work on a routine and fired her. She went into a bit of a shell after that, and her next boss fired her for not talking enough to customers.

Marlene's optimism had taken a bit of a beating and she was feeling slightly defeated by the big city when she spotted Katrina's sign looking for help. She almost didn't notice the sign as she walked past, having just come from two other interviews that didn't hold much hope. Everyone wanted five years experience and wanted her to bring a client base of at least ten regulars with her. The small 'Help Wanted' sign in the front of Kat's Kuts was written in pencil on a ten centimeter square sticky note. Marlene only saw the note when she stopped to pick up a glove she dropped from her pocket. She wasn't even aware that the place was reopening with a new owner.

When Marlene sat down to talk to Katrina, it was like she was talking to an older sister. Their backgrounds were so similar and

Katrina made her feel welcome from the moment they met. They got to know each other better in the few months she began working there, but they hadn't had many chances to just hang out. They both enjoyed the couple of 'Mystery Movie' nights at Marlene's small apartment. It was nice for Marlene to have a friend in the big city, and sharing her favourite hobby of crime solving was fun. It was a nice change from reading a mystery novel alone in bed. Her first two work experiences seemed like distant bad memories and now she loved going to work each day, just as her father did.

15   *Buying Time*

Morning came and found Katrina alone in the apartment. It wasn't a comfortable feeling for her. While she wasn't the kind of girl that needed a guy around to feel safe and secure, she always felt that way knowing Jonathan was around or would around be at some point. She didn't notice it, but she was dragging around a little slower than a normal workday. Katrina was moving quicker than a hangover day, but not by much. There definitely was some self-pity in her mind. She had just dumped her boyfriend for starters. She had just buried a customer. And there was the small issue of having to come up with $10,000 in just over a week or lose her business. As the slow trickle of warm water ran over her face in her shower, she wasn't sure what to do. Maybe the bus ride would give her some ideas, although it was highly unlikely.

Katrina got off the bus at her stop and ritualistically tossed her two quarters in the new hat of Spare Change. At least she was alert enough today to notice the new hat. She walked in the front door of the salon and with her head down she started toward the back room to hang up her coat.

"What am I today, chopped liver?" was the smart remark from Kevin, who Katrina had completely ignored as she came in.

"Oh, Kevin, I'm so sorry. I've got a lot on my mind this morning."

"So what did lover boy have to say about the bills not being paid?"

"He denied it, at least at first. Would you believe he actually tried to lie his way out of it? But I busted his sorry ass so bad."

"Good for you, Kat! Please tell me that you kicked him out!" Kevin implored, his hands clasped together like he was praying.

"Yes, I did," Katrina replied, but not boasting about it.

"Hallelujah! Is it too early to have a celebratory drink?" as he did a slight jump up and down with a small handclap thrown in for good measure.

"Sorry if I don't feel like celebrating. I've still got to deal with the financial mess that he left behind."

"I've already talked to Ron. Well, it was more like pleading. He says he'll come in about 10:00 A.M. and help you contact that Bill Owen guy to see what the damage is. He says he may have the ability to buy you some more time anyway.

"Thanks, Kevin!" and she leaned forward and gave him a big hug out of appreciation.

"I'm just thinking of my job," Kevin replied back, but he was as concerned about his friend as he was his job.

As Katrina pulled away from the hug, the salon's phone rang.

"Kat's Kuts. May I help you?" she answered the phone. She listened and recognized the voice, but not immediately.

"It's been two days," said the voice over the phone. She listened for another sentence hoping to put the name to the voice. "I said that I'd call you in two days to see if you were going to accept my offer."

"Ben!" she replied, happy that she was able to tell who it was. She was also relieved that it wasn't a bill collector or someone else with bad news. She had thought a bit on the way in to work about Ben's offer. She decided to ask him her pent-up question before replying to his question. "Did the McAllister's request that Duncan get buried in knock-off jewelry?"

"No. Why do you ask?"

"Never mind for now," and she prepared to answer his question. His answer was enough for her to want to snoop around to find out what happened to Duncan's good jewelry. She also thought that the extra money wouldn't hurt either.

"I'll do it," she stated firmly into the receiver.

"Excellent. Can you come in later today? I've got an elderly lady that needs a cut," Ben replied, not wasting any time.

"Sure. Is it okay if I bring some help? . . . Yes, I realize that we'll split the fee. . . . Okay, great. See you then," and she hung up the phone and turned to look at Kevin.

"Oh no, not me sister. I was okay when I thought it was maybe one quick gig for a good chunk of cash. But I am not interested in doing it all the time."

"It's not that bad, really," and she looked him right in the eye. "Well, okay, so maybe it's a little creepy. I really want someone to go with me to snoop around over there. I think someone is stealing the expensive jewelry from the stiffs."

"Well, normally the two terms expensive and stiff in the same sentence would suffice enough to say 'deal me in', but not in this case. Maybe little Katrina junior will help you? Why don't you ask her when she gets in?"

"I believe I will," Katrina answered to Kevin's suggestion to have Marlene help her out.

The next hour flew by. Marlene had come in and agreed to help out Katrina. She was mostly interested in the sleuthing aspect of the proposal, and went on for about thirty minutes about all the different detective books she had read and television shows she had watched. She prided herself with figuring out 'who done it' before it was revealed in the book or show. Katrina half-expected Marlene to show up at the funeral home in a trench coat and a Sherlock Holmes-style hat.

Shortly after that, Ron had shown up to itemize what was going on with the bills. He got on the phone with Bill Owens, followed by a call to the bank, another call to Bill Owens, and then an hour and a half of working in solitude. Ron had somehow managed to squeeze everything onto a very small round table in the back room. He said he had worked on people's books in worse places before. At least this table was clean.

"Well dear" Ron started his summary "it is pretty bad. I don't like using the words, but can't think of a better term — he has basically financially raped you. You have less than $100 in your joint chequing account. He cleaned out as much as the ATM would let him late last night. Kevin tells me that Jonathan's got a gambling problem. What he took last night is likely already wagered and lost. I have managed to get you an extra couple of weeks from the bill collector and bank, and convinced them to settle for half at that time, and the other half two weeks later."

"Thanks, Ron. Kevin says you're the best, and I have to agree," and she hugged Ron. As she pulled away, she finished with "But I'm still not sure that I can come up with even the half by then."

"You just call me if you have any more questions, Katrina. I'll see if I can think of anything else in the meantime."

Kevin brought Ron his coat and helped him on with it. They exchanged a short hug, and a quick peck on the cheek before Ron left.

"Don't worry, Kat. We'll figure it out," an all-too perky Marlene told her. "Is it time to go do some detective work?"

"I suppose. Kevin, Bianca should arrive soon to cover one of the chairs. Be nice to her, please!!"

16 The Snoop Sisters

The girls got on the bus and headed to the funeral home. Marlene was more talkative than usual. This made the bus ride very different for Katrina, who was used to riding in solitude.

"Slow down on your questions, Marlene."

"Sorry, I'm just excited! It's like I'm in my own mystery movie."

"Here's the scoop. I noticed at Duncan's funeral that his Gucci watch and antique pocket watch were swapped out with fakes. I talked to the funeral director, Ben, and he said that they didn't do it. So, we want to find out who stole them. The thieves may work at other funeral homes too."

"It could be a visitor to the funeral home, but in most of the movies and books it's usually an inside job. Who would you suspect?"

"I don't know yet. I've met only the funeral director, his assistant, and the doorman. Granderson, the door man, is about two hundred years old and moves slower than molasses."

"What about the other two? What clues can you give me?"

"Well Sherlock, I'm hoping you can dig up some for me."

Marlene's eyes lit up and a huge smile engulfed her face. She looked like a kid seeing the presents under the tree on Christmas morning.

"I'm your man, Kat. I mean, I'll get to the bottom of it. Leave it to me. When I'm done, I'll be able to tell you what they eat everyday and how many times they go to the bathroom."

"I was kinda hoping you'd just tell me who has been stealing the jewelry."

"That too!" replied the overly enthusiastic Marlene.

They arrived at the funeral home about 20 minutes earlier than Ben was expecting them, so Katrina skipped his office and steered Marlene to one of the visitation rooms.

"I'm going to check out the people here. See if someone looks suspicious," Marlene informed Katrina. "Could behave like an arsonist – I hear they always return to the scene of the crime."

Katrina looked perplexed at Marlene, wondering how she had come up with such an analogy.

"Good idea. Keep an eye out for people who don't look like they should be wearing expensive jewelry or for people lurking about the casket."

"Got it. See you in 20 minutes out in the entrance. Going undercover now."

Katrina rolled her eyes. What did she get herself into getting Marlene involved? Marlene's ideas were basically good, but Katrina worried about the approach. Katrina was worried Marlene would jump someone and perform a citizen's arrest in the middle of the funeral home.

Marlene slowly went from group to group, looking people over from head to foot. She'd ask specific people for the time as a ruse to see their watch. Marlene was watching people to see if they appeared 'emotionally effected' while at the funeral. She figured that the thief would appear detached and not show emotion. She was checking eyes for redness or puffiness and cheeks for signs of spilled tears.

Katrina, meanwhile, was making her way up to the casket to check out what jewelry the deceased was wearing. When she got up there, the lady's watch, three strand pearl necklace, and matching bracelet and earrings were real. No one had hit this one yet. She decided to turn her attention to the crowd where Marlene was mingling. She recognized a guy from yesterday's funeral, but just one. That likely meant that he wasn't a FRED as they tended to get hired in bunches. There were bound to be other faces she'd recognize from yesterday if FREDs were working. She decided to watch his movements for a while.

The 'suspect' was in a small group talking with two others when Katrina noticed Marlene join the group. She watched Marlene jump right into the conversation. It looked like Marlene was asking questions mostly of the man and not the others in the group. After a couple of minutes, Marlene politely nodded and separated from the group, stepping behind the man. She held up both her hands with one hand cupped to cover the pointing motion she was making with the other toward the 'suspect'. Katrina was having trouble making out what

Marlene was mouthing to her, but it looked like she was saying 'It's him.'

Katrina motioned discreetly for Marlene to come over to her, which she did.

"He doesn't seem to know anybody here. I see no sign he's been crying either." Marlene reported back on her mission.

"Not everyone cries at funerals you know, especially guys."

"I suppose, but I don't detect any emotion from this guy."

"Okay. Let's keep an eye on him," Katrina whispered to Marlene.

Marlene nodded in agreement. Just then, the guy started out of the room, toward the entrance. The girls looked at each other. He hadn't gone anywhere near the casket.

"Follow me," Marlene instructed Katrina, grabbing her arm and pulling her.

They watched the guy walk into the entrance, and look up at the signs for the other rooms. He then proceeded into one of the other visitation rooms.

"I've heard of crashing parties, but never funerals," Katrina whispered to Marlene. "We've got five minutes still. Let's just sneak past Ben's office and see what this guy's up to."

The man stood toward the back of the room and was just looking around. To appear inconspicuous, the girls decided to go up to the casket and pay their respects. Fortunately, there was no lineup, so they didn't have to engage in any conversation with other visitors, such as how they knew the deceased.

"Does everyone in this city have a Gucci or Rolex?" Marlene quipped, noticing the wrist of the deceased.

"Nice watch!" responded Katrina. "Obviously a lot of people make more money than we do. I always wonder what these guys do to have this kind of money."

"Maybe they just outlive their debts. You know, no more kids to put through university. House is paid for."

"Whatever it is, let's see if our guy makes a move."

They stood around for about five minutes, but the guy just stood at the back, before moving to a comfy chair at the side and sitting down.

"Damn," Katrina said. "We've got to go. I don't want Ben to get suspicious of our motives, or if he's the guy, we won't catch him."

"You're right. Let's go meet Ben. Besides, it will give me a chance to size him up."

They exited the visitation room and headed to Ben's office. As they approached, they caught the tail end of a conversation coming from the office. It was Ben, apparently on the phone.

"I don't care about that now. You promised me another set by today, and I haven't got it." Then, there was a moment's silence, while he listened for a response.

"I don't need excuses. I need that other set. And I need it now!" and the phone was slammed down.

The girls decided to wait in the hall a few extra seconds so he wouldn't think that they had overheard any of the conversation.

Katrina entered the room, followed closely by Marlene.

Ben looked first at Katrina, and then noticed Marlene. He looked her up and down, not noticing his mouth hanging half open. Katrina was expecting his tongue to drop out and hit the floor.

"I've really got to get down and see your salon!" Ben exclaimed.

"Easy, tiger," whispered Marlene. Katrina gave her a quick elbow to keep it quiet, afraid he'd hear her.

"This is Marlene. She's here to help me. If she handles it okay, and you're okay with it, she may come here sometimes in my place.

"Oh, by all means," Ben replied, still eyeing Marlene up and down. "Now before you start, I need to give you a quick orientation."

Marlene groaned. "What's there to learn about a funeral home and working with stiffs?"

"Well, for one, we generally don't go around calling them stiffs."

Marlene replied. "Point taken. Explain away."

"So, first of all, I am the funeral home manager, meaning everyone who works here, including you, reports to me. I am a certified funeral director. There are usually two other funeral directors here, but they are a married couple, and as I mentioned earlier, I was dumb enough to let them take a month-long trip to New Zealand in the middle of winter – our busiest season, unfortunately."

"What about Tammy?" Katrina asked.

"She's an intern. She's completed her eight months of school and is six months into her year-long internship. And we prefer to use the term 'loved one' when referring to the deceased. It is more comforting to their families. I tell all of our employees to treat our guests with the utmost respect, understanding, and privacy during their difficult time." Ben looked for an acknowledging nod from the two girls. "That should be enough to keep you out of trouble. Any questions?"

"Yeah," Marlene answered, "do you think I can drive the hearse some time? Empty, of course."

"No, I don't think so," and Ben smiled at the child like question. "And, it's called a coach."

"Thanks, Ben," Katrina said, giving Marlene a look for her question. "Now, what's the name of the nice lady we're supposed to clean up? And will you get her out for us?"

"It's Mrs. Wilmont. And Tammy will set you up down there." He turned to Marlene and continued "She's my assistant — very thorough — she's down there now."

"Thanks, Ben. We'll come up and say goodbye before we leave."

"Bye. Nice meeting you."

"You, too! Good luck."

They headed out of the office and down the hallway toward the back of the funeral home where the steps to the basement were located.

"I'm surprised he didn't drool," Katrina remarked about Ben's behaviour at the sight of Marlene.

"You just didn't notice he was trying to look down your blouse whenever you turned away from him. I think he's an equal opportunity leerer."

Katrina somehow felt better that Marlene said this. Katrina detected Ben checking her out yesterday, but thought the reaction was pale compared to how he looked at Marlene. For some bizarre reason, Katrina was slightly offended that he seemed to leer more at Marlene. It was likely due to Jonathan's complete lack of attention the past week. Or, maybe she was losing it a bit.

They made their way down the stairs and into the room where Tammy was supposed to be.

"Where is she?" Marlene asked.

"Probably in the back room. They use it when they're busy."

"Are you going to go get her?"

"Not in this lifetime! It would be like walking into a morgue. I can only deal with one body at a time. You can go get her, if you want."

"No, thanks. I'm good," replied Marlene, wrapping her arms around herself like she just got a creepy chill.

The door to the back room slowly opened like an automated handicap door. A body on a table started to emerge through the door. It was that of an elderly lady.

"Mrs. Wilmont, I presume?" Katrina said, in her best Stanley meets Livingstone impersonation. This startled Tammy, who was pushing the table.

"Oh, my god," Tammy replied, crossing her hands on her chest like she was catching her breath. "Every time I finally think I'm used to this place, I get a start like this and realize I'm still slightly creeped out by it down here."

"You can say that again!" Marlene agreed.

"And you are ???" Tammy inquired.

"I'm sorry," apologized Katrina, "this is Marlene. She's here to help me today."

"Nice to meet you, Marlene. It's better not to work alone down here anyway." Tammy turned and motioned toward the body on the table. "You are right, you have found Mrs. Wilmont. And here is a lovely picture of her . . . about 20 years ago," as she handed a photo to Katrina. "I know people want to remember their loved ones a certain way, but it would make it easier for you and me if they gave us a current photo. Look at the hair she had in this photo. You'd have to slap a wig on her to get a look like that now."

"I'm sure we'll figure something out, " Katrina said, looking at the photo before passing it over to Marlene.

"This looks like the same style my grandmother had years ago. We can just do Mrs. Wilmont's hair like my grandmother has now. Should come pretty close," Marlene answered, scrutinizing the picture.

"Pretty and smart too. You better watch she doesn't steal your business from under you," Tammy stated.

Katrina wasn't sure, but she didn't seem to detect any implied humour in the remark even though Marlene laughed at it.

"Well, I'll leave you two at it. Just let Ben know when you have finished."

The two ladies spent the next hour working on Mrs. Wilmont's hair, trying to make the dear old lady look classy one last time. As they packed up the tools of their trade, Katrina looked over at Marlene who didn't seem fazed by any of this.

Marlene put the last few items in the bag and looked back at Katrina.

"Can we get back to sleuthing now?"

17 *Takedown*

As Katrina and Marlene made their way back upstairs, they decided to see if the mystery man was still lurking about. The visitation was still in progress in the room the man was in before, so they started searching for him there.

"Look. He's still here. He's just moved to the other side of the room." Katrina nudged Marlene as she made the comment.

"Seems awfully suspicious to me."

"Me, too. Let's go back up front and see if the Rolex is still there."

They made their way up front to view the body. This time there was a slight line-up.

"How did you know my uncle?" asked a man's voice from behind.

"Pardon me?" a stunned Katrina responded.

"How did you know my uncle?" and the man motioned toward the body lying up front.

"Oh, we knew him from work," Marlene replied.

The man's eyebrows scrunched up, expressing bewilderment.

"You two worked on Toronto's Solid Waste Management crew?" The man looked the two of them up and down. "You don't really look the type."

"We actually didn't work with him . . . " Marlene tried to answer, but couldn't find a good reply.

"We knew him from his work because our uncle worked with him," Katrina jumped in.

"And where is your uncle?" the man asked looking around.

"Sadly, Uncle Jack passed away late last year. We just came to pay respects on his behalf ."

The man wasn't sure whether to believe their reason, but let it go without further discussion. The girls were now in front of the open casket, their heads bowed down pretending to pray for the departed. In actuality, they were trying to see if his watch was still there and that it was still a Rolex.

"The sleeve's now covering the watch. It wasn't like that before Katrina!"

"You're right!" Katrina gave a quick peak over her shoulder to see if the inquisitive man was lurking behind her. He was. Surely he would notice her reach into the casket to pull the deceased's sleeve up. She raised her purse up so that it was resting on the lip of the casket. She waited a few seconds, then edged the bag over and onto the deceased.

"Damn. I mean Oops. Clumsy of me." The man's nephew looked on appearing aggravated now by their presence and the hold up in the line of guests waiting to pay their respects. Katrina didn't pay attention and reached to retrieve her purse. Instead, she slid up the man's suit coat sleeve and shirt sleeve to reveal a cheap knock-off watch.

"Gone!" she said, and she picked up her purse and half pushed Marlene away from the casket. "I'm going in."

"What do you mean? You're not crawling into the casket, are you?"

"I'm going to talk to our mystery man to see if he's got a nice new Rolex adorning his arm."

"Good luck. I'll lay low."

Katrina slowly walked to the back of the room along the outside aisle of chairs on the opposite side of the room from where the man sat. She sat down and, making sure he wasn't looking, slid her watch off and put it in her purse. Katrina then got up and nonchalantly drifted over towards him. She hadn't paid that close attention to his looks earlier. As she moved toward him, she was taken aback that she hadn't noticed his striking looks and his well-built body. Granted, he was a bit rough around the edges. His hair was a little tossed and one of his shoes had come untied. He didn't look comfortable in the blazer, but the jeans that he wore fit right.

"This must be getting over soon!" she said emphatically but quietly to him, trying to sound tired of the ordeal. "Do you mind?" and she gently took his hand and pulled his arm toward her. Katrina then spun around his outreached arm, sliding herself closely in front of him while maintaining a tender grasp of his hand. Her back caressed up against his chest as she slid his blazer sleeve up his arm to reveal his watch. It was also one of her best come-on moves, and although she was a little rusty, the judges would have likely given her nines across the board.

"Uh," and then the man cleared his throat, "Not at all . . . ," not that he had a choice with Katrina's maneuver.

"Thank God!" she uttered as she stared at his watch, "only five more minutes. Do you think anyone would notice if I snuck out early?" Katrina had kicked the flirting up another notch. She almost forgot the purpose of her mission. She snapped back into focus and realized that his arm was adorned with a stunning gold Rolex. She couldn't be certain it was the same watch, but this dude didn't look like he was made of money. Muscle maybe, but money no. She now had to think of a way to slip out of her flirting position so she could get back and tell Marlene. Katrina wanted to get to Ben's office right away to report it and see what they should do next.

"Oh, dear, I forgot about my friend Marlene," and she waved over to Marlene. "She's a little slow, if you know what I mean, so I can't leave her for long. Maybe another time," and she dropped his arm and scurried across the room.

The man just stood there shell shocked. He'd blown a lot of introductions before, but this had to set a record. He didn't even get a name – not even a fake name. He stood there scratching his head.

"It's got to be him! It looks like the same watch."

"What's next?"

"I'm going to tell Ben and see what he thinks we should do."

"I don't know that we have time . . . the guy's leaving!"
Marlene was excitedly bobbing up and down on her toes. "We've got to
take him down!" she finished.

"What?"

"We've got to take him down. Stop him before he gets away
with it."

"I'm not even positive it's him."

"Yes you are. You just don't want to act. He's already in the
entrance way. He'll be gone in a minute."

Katrina thought what if this was the guy and she let him get
away? She'd kick herself all night. She tried to rationalize accusing the
man. If he wasn't the guy, they'd just apologize and go their separate
ways. Katrina's heart was pounding in her chest and a rush of adrenalin
kicked in.

"Okay. Let's go!"

The girls started half-running toward the foyer of the funeral
home. There was a bit of a crowd assembled as another funeral
procession was moving toward an awaiting coach. The six pallbearers
had lifted the casket from the bier, and Ben had rolled the bier out of the
way. The pall bearers were supporting their loved one's casket at the
front of the growing throng. They were stopped half out of the door,
with four of the pallbearers through the doorway and the last two still
positioned under the doorframe. The attendees stood about five or six
people deep, and the girls' mystery man stood in the middle about two
rows from the casket.

With Marlene leading the charge, she and Katrina began to push their way through the crowd. Pushing obviously doesn't happen every day at a funeral, so they got some annoyed looks as they ploughed forward. A lady mumbled 'must be Americans, always in a hurry'. They got to within two people of the man when the pallbearers started moving again and the front of the crowd surged forward. Finding a seam in the crowd with the surge, their man slipped through an opening in the bodies and was getting further away.

"Enough of this shit," Marlene said in frustration, and started to push her way through the crowd with renewed vigor. She never imagined while she was running all those basketball drills in high school that she'd end up boxing out people at a funeral home. Katrina simply followed in Marlene's wake.

They broke free of the crowd as it spilled outside and in the process somehow Katrina ended up in front of Marlene. Before the man could get any further, Katrina took two quick, long strides and lunged at him. Her tackle carried him into the last two pallbearers as were raising the casket in preparation for securing it in the coach. The pallbearers stumbled awkwardly, releasing their grip on the handles while falling into the next two ball bearers. The middle set of pall bearers also let go. The front ball bearers were barely holding on as they had placed the front edge of the casket on the threshold of the coach. The weight was too much for the two remaining pallbearers to hold the casket in place and it fell with a thud to the surface of the parking lot.

Ben was standing right there overseeing the loading of the casket. Again, he had seen a lot in his days as a funeral director, but this was new. He quickly ran over to the casket and did something to it, but nobody noticed what in all the commotion. He then got up and went over to Katrina.

"Just what are you doing Katrina?"

"I was about to ask the same," the man on the ground replied as he started to get up. As the man did, something fell out of the inside of his blazer onto the ground. It was a police badge.

Katrina sat there, looking up at Marlene like she intended to kill her.

"I'm sorry Katrina. I thought he was the guy."

"What are you talking about?" the officer said.

"How about we take this into my office? I think we've disrupted this family's privacy enough already," Ben emphatically stated.

"Fine with me," said the officer, offering his hand out to Katrina to help her up.

With the crowd looking all around and abuzz with what they had just seen and what they thought it was about, the four proceeded back into the building. Katrina was shivering a bit on the way. In the haste, she had gone outside without a coat and was wet from landing in the combination of light snow and slush that covered the surface of the parking lot.

"Here. You look cold," and the officer took off his blazer and put it over Katrina's shoulders. She smiled back at him, wondering why he would act so nice after what she had done. "My name's Jake, by the way."

"So, what's this all about then?" asked Ben.

"It's my fault, so let me explain," Marlene responded.

"No, it's my fault. I'll explain," Katrina interrupted. "You know how I asked you about Duncan's jewelry the other day? Well, someone stole his good stuff sometime between the time I cut his hair and when I saw him at the funeral. So we were playing detective today and noticed that the watch disappeared from the deceased in the Heaven's Gate room. This man here, I mean Officer Jake, looked like he had the same watch. And nothing personal, but you don't look like the type that can afford a Rolex, or the kind of guy that would even wear one."

"Well you're right about that. Most police officers don't sport Rolex's on our salaries. But this was a gift from my parents when I made detective. Don't wear it much, actually, but thought it would dress me up and make me look less suspicious today."

"Turns out it made you more suspicious," Marlene chirped in.

"So what are you doing here anyway?" Katrina asked, changing the subject slightly.

"I'm working. We've had three complaints about missing belongings this month from family members. They didn't want to notify you Mr. Better, in case you were involved."

"Understood," Ben acknowledged.

"And did you find out anything?" Marlene queried.

"I've got a few leads but now my cover's blown, thanks to Big Ben Baker here," referencing the Argonaut's football player.

Katrina blushed, recalling her earlier escalator episode with the real Big Ben Baker.

"It *was* a good tackle," Marlene said.

"Don't go there . . . " Katrina threatened, still upset with her impulsive actions.

Jake looked at Katrina, but hesitated before speaking. He was temporarily tongue-tied as he captured his first deep gaze into her alluring green eyes. "If you think you're embarrassed, think how I'm going to feel when I have to explain this to my boss."

18 *Questions*

The next day at work Katrina and Marlene rehashed the events from their episode at the funeral home. Both felt embarrassed by the takedown of Jake, although Katrina felt slightly more so because he was cute and she thought he was coming on to her. Although she was only a few days removed from her breakup with Jonathan — and she shouldn't really think about getting into another relationship — there was something about Jake that she couldn't get out her mind. For one, he struck her as an old-fashioned gentleman. But then she recalled Jonathan had started out that way too. Jake had a certain ruggedness that did something for her. It was a stark contrast to Jonathan's polished exterior. She told herself that she had to stop comparing Jake to Jonathan. Having to listen to girlfriends compare current boyfriends to former boyfriends was a pet peeve of hers. She didn't see the point in it. You can always find fault in someone if you look hard enough (former boyfriends), and you can always ignore faults if you don't want to see them (current boyfriends).

"At least we were right about the crimes going down, even if we tagged the wrong guy for it," an optimistic Marlene said as she swept up from the her previous customer.

"Yeah, you're right. Jake wouldn't have been there if we weren't on to something."

"So you agree we need to go back and snoop around some more!"

"I don't think so, at least not just yet."

"Why wait? I thought you were supposed to 'strike while the iron is hot', although I always thought that branding cows was inhumane."

"I think I'm going to take a more direct approach. I'm going to talk directly to Ben about it, and see if he's got ideas about who's involved."

"I'm sure Jake did that yesterday after we left."

"You're likely right, but I think Ben may open up more to me. For one, I'm not a complete stranger and I'm not the police."

"And you've got breasts for Ben to stare at, which Jake doesn't, although Jake did look like he worked the upper body."

Ben seemed tickled that Katrina would ask him out for lunch. He gladly accepted the short notice invitation, not that Ben had to clear his calendar or anything as he usually ate lunch at this desk anyway. She had arranged to meet him at a small place just down the block from her salon, since she figured he had a car and could get there easier than her taking the bus someplace. Marlene begged to go as she channeled her inner Sherlock Holmes. Katrina finally convinced her that Ben might feel like he was in front of the Spanish Inquisition if they both started firing questions at him.

Katrina arrived at the restaurant before Ben and was seated with a soft drink in her hand before he appeared. After a bit of polite chitchat about the weather and traffic, she asked him her first question.

"So, did the officer grill you with questions yesterday?"

"A bit I suppose. It's not like he held a hot white spotlight over my head and screamed at me like you see in some movies. Then again, I don't have a spotlight in my office."

"You never know. After all, you do have cameras in your morgue. Did he accuse you of the thefts?"

"No, not at all. He said I'm not totally clear of being a suspect but I'm really low on his list. He highly doubts I'm his guy. Some of his questions were kind of strange though."

"Like what?"

"Mostly he asked about you."

"Me? Does he think I'm a suspect? I mean, does he think I would tackle him like that if I was the thief?"

"No, he mostly asked what I knew about you. Like where you worked, how often you came by the funeral home to work, if you were single. It was personal stuff, not like a crime investigation."

Katrina was slightly blushing. She was happy to know that he seemed taken by her too. "So what'd you tell him?"

"I told him the name of your salon, that you were 'on call' for the funeral home, and that anything else he'd have to talk to you in person. I have no intention of playing matchmaker."

"Yes, of course." Katrina sensed that Ben seemed a little put off by the attention that Jake was paying her. She was concerned he was going to clam up, so she decided to resort to an old trick from Cathy. She took the menu and lightly waved it over her chest like it was hot in the place. She undid her top blouse button to reveal some cleavage. While she wasn't endowed anything like Cathy, it still did the trick. She noticed Ben sit up immediately, likely trying to get a better view. Now she could proceed with her questions.

"What do you think of Tammy? She doesn't seem thrilled about working at a funeral home."

"She's not. I think she's okay; her work is fine. She is a little ambitious at times and I think she might have designs on my job. I can't see her as the type to steal watches and pawn them though."

"Me neither. Isn't she really over qualified for the job she's doing? Why do you think she's working at a funeral home when she doesn't like it and is overqualified."

"You know, she was really keen during her intern interview, bubbly and enthusiastic. I was mostly concerned about the job being beneath her talents, but she'd done her schooling and was desperate for the job. Her resume had some company name that I didn't recognize for her last job. I asked her about it and she said it was a personal business venture that had failed. She wanted to work for somebody for a while instead of trying to run the whole show. She seemed very sincere about the whole thing."

"I'm sure she's okay. Is there anyone else around there that you think might be involved? I got the impression from the officer that he thought it might be an inside job." She was careful not to use Jake's name, in case it ruffled Ben's feathers again. She was too shy to undo another button on her blouse. "Some of the guys seem a little shady."

"You mean like Larry, the coach driver? We are a small funeral home by Toronto standards. We're more the size of places in smaller cities like Windsor or London. I can't afford to buy a coach, so we rent one from this place that does that for a few of the other smaller places too. I'm not sure why, but we tend to end up with Larry more often than not. He prefers to go by Lawrence by the way – thinks it makes him sound more distinguished. Big ego. Kind of slimy. When he sees you, you'll probably hear more bad pickup lines in five minutes than you've heard your whole life. And I'm sure you've heard a lot!"

Katrina blushed and instinctively put her hand over the area of the recently undone button. "Oh great! Gives me something to look forward to."

"And then we have the Star Wars twins."

"The what?"

"Hans and Darth. Their dad was a certified Star Wars geek. Lived and breathed it. I think he disappeared when they were ten. He apparently told his wife that he had a secret mission on Alderaan and might not return. He didn't."

"Can't wait to meet them."

"Hans comes in only part-time, when we are really busy. But Darth's a full-time funeral assistant and actually lives upstairs in a small apartment that years ago was the home of the funeral home manager. I let him live there rent free in exchange for paying him minimum wage instead of a regular salary."

"Anyone else worth mentioning?"

"We get a number of different people delivering flowers to the home, but there's a guy Ned from the place around the corner that's there nearly every day. We recommend them to people who ask since they are so conveniently located."

"Is that it for people who work at Shady Rest?"

"And, of course, there's me."

"Yes, you. So tell me about yourself . . . " Katrina thought she might pick up a clue or two if she let Ben babble about himself. But mostly she wanted to eat and figured she could squeeze a few grunts of acknowledgement in while she had her roasted chicken salad.

After 20 minutes of Ben's story telling— which contained no clues whatsoever but did have a few humourous moments — there was finally a break of silence.

"Oh, by the way" Ben continued, "I forgot to tell you that I've got another job for you today. That is, if you can?"

"I suppose I can clear my afternoon." Katrina thought this was a good chance to talk to some of the other people who worked there. "Can I get a ride back with you?"

"Okay, but I'll take the bus fare off your pay."

"Really?"

"No, just joking!"

Katrina was relieved because he seemed like the type who would do it. After all, he didn't offer to pay for lunch and his tip was a collection of small loose coins that couldn't have added up to much more than a dollar.

19   *Flower Power*

After an uneventful, and even bordering on boring, car ride back from lunch, Katrina and Ben pulled into the parking lot of the funeral home. It was early in the afternoon and there were no visitors yet. Just the employees were present doing their set-up jobs, etc.

     She excused herself from Ben and headed to the ladies' room. Upon exiting, Katrina headed into one of the visitation rooms. There was a guy there setting up flowers. She browsed at some of the arrangements, smelling a few as she made her way over to him. He was tidying up a bouquet he had just brought in from his delivery van.

     "Hello," she said to get his attention, since his back was still toward her. As he turned, Katrina noticed he was conveniently wearing a golf-style shirt with the floral company's name on the right side of the chest and 'Ned' embroidered on the left pocket. Her eyes moved up toward his face. If he had won any beauty contests as a baby, they must have been judged by his mother. His facial complexion was pock-marked and his nose resembled the oversized red nose of an alcoholic. She didn't take sport in teasing guys like some girls she knew. She'd rather politely express disinterest than string along some guy in a bar for the sake of a free drink or two or three. Regardless of her lack of interest, Katrina was on a mission and put herself in flirting gear.

"Hello, Ned. My name is Katrina," and she extended a hand to shake. "I just started working here, so we'll likely see a lot of each other."

"Pleased to meet you, Katrina. I'm sure you weren't named after the hurricane. I mean, you would have been born before that, and, ah, not to say you look like a hurricane hit you or anything . . . "

Smooth, Katrina thought. His babbling almost had her looking forward to listening to Lawrence's obnoxious lines, but not quite.

"That's okay. I know what you mean. I was actually named after a porcelain doll that my mother had when she was a girl. Were you named after someone?"

"My dad, actually. But I don't like to go by Ned Jr. or Junior. You are pretty like a doll."

Katrina smiled, amazed at how terrible Ned was at flirting. She also noticed that he was constantly sniffling. Could this loner be a coke nose?

"Thank you, Ned. That's very sweet."

"You know, most girls don't talk to me."

Katrina could only image why.

"I think they think I'm gay because I work at a flower shop."

That likely didn't help, Katrina thought. His communication skills might have something to do with it too.

"Sorry about the sniffling. I'm allergic to roses."

Katrina wondered why a guy with an allergy to roses would work at a flower shop, but decided to not bother asking.

"Say, Ned, that's a nice watch that you've got there," noticing the nice Gucci on his wrist. She wondered about his reason for having such a pricey watch.

"It is, isn't it? I bought it from Lawrence, the driver. Only a hundred bucks! He says he has lots of them. He said something about buying them in bulk. Said he takes a loss on the individual watch, but makes it up in volume. I don't understand that high-finance stuff myself. Lawrence though, he's the high-roller type. He gets all that. Have you met him yet?"

"No, I haven't had the pleasure. I hope to soon though. He sounds really interesting. It was nice talking to you, Ned. I've got to run and go cut and style some hair."

Perhaps, finally a clue Katrina thought as she walked out into the hallway.

A woman in her fifties approached Katrina.

"Excuse me. Can I have a word with you?"

"I'm sorry. Do I know you?" Katrina asked.

"No, I don't think so. I'm Mrs. Wilmont's daughter. I wanted to say how lovely you made her hair look." A tear rolled down the lady's face.

"You're welcome. I'm sorry for your loss."

"That's what I want to talk to you about, my loss. Can we go somewhere private?"

"Sure. I think one of the visitation rooms is empty right now. Is that okay?"

"Yes, that's fine."

The lady followed Katrina into the room, looking behind her as she entered.

"I've noticed you doing some private investigation work and I'd like to hire you."

"But I'm not a private eye."

"You could have fooled me. Besides, I don't know whom to trust. I want to go to the police, but my mother never trusted the police and I'm honoring her wishes."

"So, what can I do for you?"

"A number of jewelry items disappeared from my Mother's casket - heirlooms that can't be replaced, a gold necklace with a small fortune in diamonds and a matching bracelet, a diamond broach, and as I've overheard you say, her watch. We feel so stupid. We only put the jewelry on for show. We wanted to impress some people. We were going to take them right back afterward."

"I'm not sure how I can help."

"Just continue to snoop around. I have faith you'll figure it out. I'm not sure why, but I do. And I'll give you $5,000 when the items are returned."

"Five thousand?" Katrina paused thinking about how desperately she could use that money.

"I'm sorry. I see I've offended you. Would $6,000 be more appropriate?"

"Oh no, $5,000 is fine." There goes Katrina's do-gooder sense going off – never able to say no.

"Great. I'll come by tomorrow with photos of the items. Here's my number if you have questions or find the items." The lady handed Katrina a business card, smiled, turned, and walked away.

Great, indeed, thought Katrina. Now she had someone depending on her to figure all this out. But the money could buy her some time with her creditors. She put the card into her purse, paused for a second to remember where she was headed, then proceeded toward the back stairs. She also regained her train of thought. This Lawrence guy is starting to sound more and more like the type to rip people off and move the watches and jewelry. She had to figure out how to get him to tip his hand. She knew that getting to talk to Lawrence would pose no problem since Ben told her the guy fashioned himself a lady's man. She had to figure out how to gain Lawrence's confidence to find out what he was really up to. Katrina reached for the handle of the door to the stairs. Instead, the door flung open, startling her and sending her falling back.

"My turn to spook you I guess," laughed Tammy Parker.

"You got me alright. How are you today?"

"I need a drink."

"Why, what's going on?"

"The usual. But I always need a drink. You up for one? After you're done in here, of course."

"Sure. Sounds good." Katrina really wanted to talk to Lawrence, but this seemed like the perfect opportunity to find out what

Tammy Parker was all about. A few drinks between girls would likely loosen Tammy's tongue a little. Katrina would just have to make sure she didn't get hammered, make a fool of herself, and forget to ask any questions. Or worse yet, not remember the answers given to the questions!

"Great! What do you need, about an hour or so?"

"Sure. That should do it. I'll come find you when I'm done. I'll want you to put the body back anyway."

"Okay. I'll show you how to put the loved ones back too."

"No, I'm good. You can do that!"

20   *Drinks, anyone?*

Katrina opened the door to Tammy's Volkswagen Beetle and got in. It was one of the newer models in a standout orange with pink and yellow flowers decorating the outside. It was a cute car, but not the type she had pictured for Tammy after their first meeting. She pictured her with something more aggressive, like a black Camaro or Mustang. Tammy got in and buckled up, carefully checked her mirrors, and backed out of her parking space at the rear of the funeral home.

"So, where are we off to?" asked Katrina, partly out of curiosity and partly to start conversation.

"A little place I hang out sometimes after work called 'Jazz it Up!'. I'm not one for the roadhouse bars. I like someplace where I can hear some good music, yet still have a conversation."

"Sounds nice. I've heard of it but never been."

"I hope you like it. The men usually act more like gentlemen than the beer guzzlers that usually hit on me at the roadhouses."

"Likely better off too."

"Definitely. The drink prices are a bit high, but the atmosphere is worth it."

Only a few minutes had gone by and they were pulling up to park at a lot beside the club. Tammy got her parking voucher from the attendant and they cut through the lot.

"Remind me to get this stamped at the bar. Otherwise they charge $20 to park. I try to get it stamped before I start drinking so I don't forget."

"Smart," as Katrina held the door open for Tammy to enter. "Where to?"

"I like to sit over there," and she pointed to a few tables just off to the side of a small stage in a larger room past the bar. "It's quiet right now and a great spot when the musicians start."

After getting her parking pass validated, the girls walked to the other room talking as they went.

"So I assume they play jazz music," Katrina said, trying to get some conversation going.

"Good guess. Do you have any favourites? They have a pretty stacked jukebox."

"Sorry, I don't know much about jazz. Actually, I know almost nothing."

"Nothing? No songs? No artists?"

"Is there a band named Flip Korea?"

"Chick Corea. And he's a pianist, not a band."

"Yeah, him. Don't know any of his music, but heard his name. By the way, what's smooth jazz? And what do they call it when it's not smooth jazz? Crunchy jazz?"

"What?"

"You know, like peanut butter. There's smooth and there's crunchy."

"You are funny, Katrina! No, it's not like that. Let me put some music on before we sit down." Tammy plunked a few quarters into the jukebox, pressed a few buttons and turned to Katrina. "These should provide a good introduction."

The girls sat down and were immediately met by a waitress who took their drink order. Tammy smiled and commented "Another thing I like – good waitresses. Those roadhouses all seem to hire twenty-one-year olds busting out of their tops. Why would I want to compete with that? Not to mention the guys in those places see those girls as how all women should be."

"Yeah, those guys aren't looking for stimulating conversation, are they?"

"I get enough leering at from Ben at work. He doesn't even try to hide that he's staring at my breasts or my ass. At least he doesn't drool."

"I know what you mean. I didn't notice until Marlene pointed it out to me. Then I watched him when Marlene was talking. He wasn't looking at her eyes. So why do you put up with it, Tammy?"

"He's actually a pretty decent boss. He's flexible with the hours that I come and go and seems to listen to my ideas. The pay could be better, but hey, it's like that on any job, isn't it?"

"I'm sure it's just coincidence that you mention pay as the drinks arrive. I'll get the first round," teased Katrina. She handed the waitress the money and a generous tip.

"Nice tip."

"I used to pay the bills as a waitress, so I know that's how they make their money. Besides, I don't want to be like that old joke."

"What old joke?"

"What's the difference between a Canadian and a canoe?"

"Give."

"Canoes tip. It was told to me by an American customer one time. Funny thing was he tipped only about 5 percent."

"So how do tips rate in the hair stylist business?"

"Not bad. It varies wildly by client. Some think if they drop a loonie on your counter for a $10 haircut that they're Bill Gates. Others will tip you $30 on a $90 perm – and give you a bonus at Christmas. That's why you need regulars in my business. They tend to treat you good."

"We don't get much repeat business in the funeral business. Maybe we should take to burying cats. They'd come back nine times!" Tammy smiled at her own joke and then turned her head slightly toward the bar. As she did, the waitress immediately picked up on it and lifted her hand making a circular motion with one finger, asking Tammy if she wanted another round. Tammy nodded and turned back to Katrina.

"So, I hear that you used to be in business for yourself too?" inquired Katrina.

"Yes. It didn't work out though. My partner . . . well he was my partner in more than business. Unfortunately, he ended up screwing me at work too. I went away for the weekend to visit my folks and when I came home he had cleared out all his stuff from the apartment."

"Oh, I'm sorry to hear that."

"It gets worse. When I got into the office Monday morning, he had cleared out a bunch of files. After a few calls, I found out that he had taken over 75 percent of my clients and was starting a new company on his own. I didn't have enough clients left to keep going. And, of course, he took all of the big clients too. He didn't touch any money, but I didn't have enough capital to buy time to basically start all over. I took the money that I could get out of the business and decided to find something where I wasn't the boss anymore, at least for now."

"I can certainly relate. My boyfriend was my financial manager. He's been ripping me off for months and has left me broke and likely to lose my business. I just want to kill the bastard."

"We have more in common than I would have ever thought," Tammy replied.

Katrina wasn't exactly sure what to make of that comment. Tammy likely meant that their personalities were so different that she didn't think they'd have much in common. No matter, she wasn't going to dwell on it. Katrina did think that Tammy's prior comment about 'at least for now' was interesting. Maybe Ben was right. Maybe Tammy was out for his job. But Katrina's gut told her no. She sympathized with

Tammy alright. Katrina didn't think that Tammy had anything sinister planned. Perhaps another round of drinks would reveal more information . . .

21   *Opening*

There was a gust of wind just as Kevin unlocked and opened the steel door to the salon for the morning. The door slammed heavily against the wall, but fortunately nothing broke. The last thing that Katrina would need right now was a bill to fix the door.

Kevin often opened up early, as Ron had to drop him off on his way to work. Kevin knew that it made Katrina feel better anyways when she came in to a lighted store. He was very fond of Katrina, of course not in a romantic way. He was flattered that Katrina had searched for him for the job. He'd always been the hunter instead of the hunted when it came to jobs. He hadn't been disappointed about quitting his other job and starting at Kat's Kuts, in spite of the initial hesitancy that often accompanies such a move. Katrina and Marlene treated him like one of the girls, and he thought of them like sisters, although Marlene was the sister who sometimes got under his skin.

The news of Jonathan's stealing from Katrina was upsetting but not surprising to Kevin. He didn't like Jonathan from the get-go. There was something about Jonathan that Kevin didn't trust. Maybe it was

Jonathan's obvious homophobia. Kevin was just glad that Katrina had the guts to stand up to Jonathan and dump his sorry ass. He'd seen too many nice guys and girls stick in loser relationships like that just because they didn't have the courage to leave.

But the financial mess that Jonathan had left Katrina in was very upsetting. He had talked to his partner about coming up with the money, but got a big 'No'. It's not that Ron didn't like Katrina, after all he did take time away from work to help buy her some time to repay her debts. But Ron stated that he didn't want to get into the salon business, and figured that's what any bail out would equate to. Kevin gauged Ron's expressions and tone and knew that this was one time not to push the 'our money' concept.

Kevin didn't have any savings of his own to speak of. He had a small bit of RRSP savings. But Kevin always figured the retirement money wouldn't be there when he was old and gray. He always thought of it as an emergency unemployment fund. It wasn't enough to cover Katrina's debts anyway.

What also worried Kevin was Katrina's obsession with the goings on down at the Shady Rest funeral home. For one, it seemed like he'd hardly seen her the last few days. For another, he was still opening up every day, yet now she was asking him to close all the time too. He didn't mind so much but he was starting to feel a little run down. Kevin thought she should focus on saving her business instead of playing private eye. He was afraid that she had already given up hope of coming up with the money and the funeral home was a convenient diversion for her.

For now, he decided to just keep plugging along, helping out wherever he could. Perhaps a miracle would happen, or he could convince Ron to change his mind. Kevin decided to buy some lottery tickets, as those 14 million to one odds seemed pretty good in comparison to his other chances.

22 *Smooth Operator*

Katrina woke up feeling like a John Deere tractor had run over her head. It was a strange analogy possibly for most people, but Katrina knew the feeling from when she was young and visiting her grandparents' farm. She was lucky to have suffered only a few scrapes and bruises. This time, the damage was all internal – brain cells only. Why did she have to have that last drink? She probably would have been okay if not for the last drink. She remembered that as the punch line from an old joke that her father used to tell, but couldn't focus enough to recall how it started. Oh, who was she trying to kid? She likely had two or three too many for her tolerance level. Thank goodness for the TTC as Tammy was in no shape to drive by the end of the night.

Katrina had a shower to try and clear the cobwebs, but that did the trick only for a few minutes. She was glad that Jonathan was gone as his hangover cure was a disgusting potion of beer, two eggs, Alka-Seltzer, and milk. It tasted as bad as it sounds. She was going to settle on good old Tylenol and water, lots and lots of water. She'd likely pee all day, but it beat the hangover.

Katrina thought about calling in sick, but when you're the boss it's not that easy. Besides, she'd left Kevin hanging a few times lately and felt like she'd been taking advantage of his friendship. She'd have to leave her talk with Lawrence until after she closed up shop for the day.

It was a fairly routine day at the salon. Katrina went out of her way to pay attention to Kevin and do some of his usual tasks — like sweeping up for him — as her way of saying thanks. Kevin wasn't complaining about the reduction in chores. During a break in the stream of customers, Katrina talked to Kevin while she cleaned.

"I really appreciate you not complaining about the sleuthing."

"Well now that you mention it, darling . . . "

"It's not just a diversion any more. That's what I want to tell you. I got a reward offered to me for recovering some priceless heirlooms."

"Priceless? Must be a good reward!"

"Priceless to the owners. Expensive yes, but not what you think of priceless."

"So how much is the reward?"

"Five thousand! But I have to recover the stuff first."

"That would put a nice dent in your debt, sweetie."

"At this point, I'm running out of options. That's why I'm spending so much time on this."

"So don't you feel bad about leaving early. Just let me know in the morning, that's all I ask. You go girl – go solve the crime, save your salon!"

"Our salon, Kevin, our salon."

At the end of the day, Katrina locked up and headed to the bus stop to start her trip to the funeral home.

Entering the funeral home, she headed to the back to the employees lounge, such as it was. Lounge was a misnomer. Employee closet would be a better label as it wasn't much bigger than a closet. It barely held a small table and two chairs. There was a small beaten-up bar fridge with a micro-sized microwave sitting directly on top. Tammy had told her that the microwave took ten minutes to make a Kraft Dinner cup instead of the 90 seconds on the instructions. And it still came out lukewarm and crunchy.

As she entered the room, she saw Lawrence. He sat slouched in his driver's tux, sunglasses on, and reading the *Toronto Sun*. Or, at least he was looking at the pictures. He slowly and coolly lifted the sunglasses above his eyes so they came to rest on his slicked back black hair. He looked her up and down twice. He cleared his throat and attempted a deep seductive voice.

"Well, you must be Katrina. I heard you were attractive, but obviously words can hardly come close to capturing your beauty."

"And you must be Lawrence. I think people understated a few things about you as well." Katrina meant one thing and Lawrence vainly took it another way. She reached out her hand to shake.

Lawrence stood up from his chair and reached out for her hand. Instead of shaking it, he held her hand and bent down to kiss it.

"The honour is most certainly mine, Mademoiselle."

As he did this, his right arm was exposed to show not one, but two Rolexes.

"My, don't you have expensive taste in watches?"

"I believe in enjoying the finer things in life my lady. I appreciate beauty, such as yourself."

Katrina tried to keep from laughing at his lines and keep to her questioning.

"But why two watches?"

"I don't mean to boast . . . " he said, in a boastful way, "but I received these watches from a set of beautiful twin lady acquaintances who gave them to me as a gift."

"Was it your birthday?"

"No, they were a thank you for an entire night and day of incredible pleasure that Lawrence bestowed upon the two of them."

"Wow, twins. That's quite a feat." Katrina wanted to see how far this guy would go with his story. She was amazed that he talked about himself in the third person.

"Yes. They were quite the pair. But I had to end it. Lawrence is a one woman man, and Lawrence didn't think it was fair to pick one over the other."

"That was very noble of Lawrence." Now he had her doing it.

"Noble. I like that expression. Yes, it was very noble, wasn't it?"

Katrina could not believe this guy. He was so full of shit that he likely could make a manure pile to rival any cattle farm.

"Ned tells me that you got him a watch really cheap."

"Ned's mouth is bigger than his little brain."

"I was just thinking that you might have a ladies watch that I could see some time."

"Maybe. Let me see what I can come up with. In the meantime, maybe we can hit the clubs sometime. Lawrence is quite the dancer, you know."

Although she was disgusted by what she was going to say, Katrina wanted to lead this guy on in hopes that he'd eventually spill his guts about stealing jewelry from the bodies. So, she crossed her fingers behind her back, like she used to do when lying to her mother, leaned forward, and in a sexy voice told him "Well, Lawrence, perhaps sometime you can earn a watch from me." She thought she was going to vomit, but caught only a taste in her mouth.

Lawrence didn't know what to say. He looked like a poker player who was holding a hand of crap cards, Jack-high, and just had his bluff called.

"Uh, yeah, maybe . . . . baby." He tried to cover his stuttering and regain his composure.

Katrina turned to head out of the lounge and looked over her shoulder to see him staring at her ass and practically drooling on himself.

"See you soon, Lawrence," and out she went. She headed directly to the bathroom where she took a damp cloth and held it to her forehead to get rid of her nauseous feeling. After that performance maybe she should go into acting in one of Cathy's plays.

Katrina decided to call Marlene to come down and help out. Ben had given Katrina another job and she thought that Marlene could help with the work and the snooping. After Marlene arrived, they both headed to the basement to work.

"Ben told me that because they are busy today, they had to move a couple of the caskets back here to make room for other visitations. So we have to go into the back room today to get the body, and move a couple of the caskets around," instructed Katrina.

"One body at a time is bad enough, I don't know if I can handle a whole room full," Marlene took a couple steps back as she made the comment.

"It's not like they're all lying around on operating tables back there. You can't see them because they are in closed caskets anyway. Although I will agree that it's creepy in a morgue kind of way, but not in a *Night of the Living Dead* kind of way."

"How about I wait out here?"

"C'mon. Don't be a baby," and Katrina held her hand and led her through the caskets and into the back room. "Okay, Mrs. Perkins. Where are you hiding?"

"Isn't this Mrs. Wilmont's casket? I remember the especially ornate handles and how gorgeous the wood was. Wouldn't it make a great hardwood floor Kat?" Marlene caressed the outside wood of the casket. As she continued stroking along the side of the casket, she brushed up against one of the bronze handles. Her thin, gold bracelet got caught on the handle and snapped off, falling to the floor underneath the casket.

"Shit. Cheap bracelet."

"I'll get it for you," and Katrina bent down to pick up the wayward jewelry. One knee went down on the floor as she reached to pick it up. The bracelet had made its way slightly under the casket. As Katrina went to get up, she cracked her head on the outside of the casket.

"Fu . . . ." Katrina let out in pain.

But that wasn't the end of it. The side of the casket had somehow popped up in the air, and fell heavily back down on the back of her head.

23 Sides

Katrina woke up to a bright light shining in her eyes. A figure hovered above her, but she was too groggy to clearly make out who it was, especially with the white light in her eyes. She assumed it was Marlene.

"My head is friggin' killing me," she moaned. "Can you help me up, gorgeous?"

"Sure. And thanks," came a man's voice.

Katrina could hear Marlene giggling in the background. Shit, Katrina thought, still unable to fully open her eyes. All she needed was to encourage Ben when he was already eyes all over her. She felt a strong, masculine hand firmly grip her hand and easily lift her toward him. Katrina was a little wobbly and grabbed on around his waist. She was suddenly in a last dance of the night kind of close to her rescuer. Her eyes opened a bit more.

"Jake!" she squealed in alarm, turning beet red at the same instant. She started to pull away instinctively. Unfortunately, her sense of balance hadn't returned. She stumbled slightly, once again getting pulled too comfortably close to the well-built detective.

"Can I just sit down for a minute?" Katrina quietly asked him. He obliged and gingerly escorted her over to a chair along the wall. Marlene sat beside her to make sure she didn't drop over.

"Are you okay, Kat?" Marlene asked as she gently held her hand. "Do you want some water or a wet cloth?"

But Jake was one step ahead of Marlene. He'd already gone to the nearby sink and was returning with a cold, damp cloth and cup of water. He handed the drink to Marlene to hold and pressed the cloth against the back of Katrina's head.

"Sorry, but there's no ice down here. I'll go up and get some once your face returns to its normal colour."

Great Katrina thought – she probably looked like hell. As if her first impression wasn't bad enough. Now the second impression was turning into a nightmare. She thought she felt something in that short embrace, but she had just suffered a blow to the head – twice. "Thanks. You're an angel . . . I meant Marlene; you're an angel for holding me up here. So, what happened?"

"You hit your head," Jake replied.

"I know that part. I mean after that."

"Take a look," motioned Marlene, pointing to the casket. The side was hanging onto the casket on one end, with the corner of the other end sitting firmly on the ground.

"What the heck?" and Katrina exclaimed. "It looks like it comes off completely."

"It does," answered Jake, easily picking up the slab of wood and reattaching it to the side. He then removed it completely and sat it on the ground.

Marlene watched Jake and whispered to Katrina "Do you know how heavy that is? Nice pipes."

Jake flipped it over to reveal a set of clips that matched the hooks on the casket.

"Look here," Jake knelt down, pointing to similar hooks holding up the ends. There were also a set of large, hand turnable screws at each end. They were likely secured only when they were going to lift the casket.

"The whole mahogany outside comes off!" exclaimed an excited Marlene.

"Maybe you can use it for a hardwood floor after all," Katrina joked.

"What do you think this is all about?" Marlene asked Jake.

"My guess is that they're selling this super deluxe Royal Mahogany casket to customers then taking off the sides before burial and reusing the sides. Nice little scam someone's got going, don't you think?"

"They must pocket a couple grand on each casket. Those things aren't cheap." Katrina answered, like she really knew.

"And that would add up over a year," added in Marlene.

Jake proceeded to put the side back on the casket, making sure it locked in snugly.

"So, who do you ladies think is behind this?" he asked as he bent over, back toward them and dusted off his knees from kneeling.

"Good question. I think we have more detective work to do." Katrina replied, all the while checking out his butt. "But let's back up a minute first," she continued, the cobwebs moving out of her head. "What are you doing here anyway, besides rescuing damsels in distress, that is?"

"When is the funeral for this person?" Jake asked ignoring her question for now, and tapping on the top of the casket, not knowing who was inside.

"Mrs. Wilmont's funeral is tomorrow. And you didn't answer my question," Katrina informed him.

"I need an inside man, I mean woman. I need someone who knows some things about the people here and that I know is on my side – at least when they're not tackling me. What do you think?"

"Sounds great!" Katrina excitedly accepted while slightly blushing over the tackle remark. Time with the hot cop sounded like just the cure for the Jonathan blues.

"What do you think of a stakeout tomorrow? I know you've been snooping around, so you can fill me in while we're waiting"

"I'd love it," Marlene chimed in.

"Sorry. I had a small mountain of paperwork to get Katrina okayed to get involved in the case. I can't afford to have two civilians at risk at a stakeout."

Katrina's eyes popped wide open. "What do you mean, *at risk*?"

24 *Distracted*

The dressing room was full of chatter as it was after all games, win or lose. This was just a men's Rec league. It was stocked with fairly good hockey players, almost all of who realized the NHL dream was gone. Of course, there were always a few jerks that played like there were scouts in the stands watching them. They were the same guys that would mix it up after every stoppage in play. Jake just got used to ignoring their shouts of 'You Wanna Go!?'

Jake was happy that it was a regular season Rec league game and not the NHL. He truly sucked out there today. His concentration was off and it showed in his play. He kept thinking about Katrina and ended up turning over the puck repeatedly. There was something about her that was different, in a good way.

"Hey, Jakester!" came a call out from across the room.

"What, Animal?"

"You sucked out there today man!"

"You noticed, eh?"

"Who didn't man? If my ex sucked like that, we'd still be married."

"I doubt it, dude. I think it had more to do with you dating other women when you were married."

"Hey, it is not my fault that chicks dig me!"

Another guy between them piped up.

"That reminds me of some dumb blonde jokes."

"What do you mean by that?" Animal glared back.

"Relax Animal, he's just jealous," Jake interrupted to calm him.

"Anyway, why did the two blondes hang out at the funeral home?"

Jake thought of Katrina and Marlene at Shady Rest.

"Because they heard there were a lot of stiff ones there."

"Got another one," a different guy yelled.

"What do you call a young blonde looking at an old guy in a casket? Wealthy!"

"How did the blonde die at the funeral home? She thought the crematory was a tanning bed."

"As much as I'd like to hear the next thousand jokes you guys have lined up, I'm outta here. See you next week." Jake grabbed his bag and sticks and headed out the dressing room door. He made his way past the player benches that were now occupied by two other teams.

"Hey Jake, wait up!" came a call from Gary who was trying to catch up from the dressing room. "You gonna stick around and scout this game? We play the red team next week."

"No, not tonight Gary."

"How 'bout a beer then? We can just grab one here at the bar."

"I think I'll just head home."

"C'mon, just one. You can hold me to it. I've got to get home by eleven or Karen will kill me."

"All right. One it is."

They dropped their gear outside the bar doors and headed in.

"So, how's the new detective job going? We miss you on the streets."

"Okay, I guess. It's hard to believe it's been six months already."

"Yeah, hard to believe. Who'd they team you with when Callaghan went out with that appendix last week?"

"It's been two weeks, and nobody. They had no one to spare, so they've stuck me on some low-risk jewelry thefts at a funeral home."

"So, what's it like as a detective? I've been thinking of trying it myself."

"It's okay. Except a couple of undercover gigs that were different than I expected."

"Like what?"

"Can't say really. You know, confidential stuff." It wasn't really, but Jake was embarrassed by it and thought this would keep Gary from asking any more questions.

"I got it. Cloak and dagger stuff."

"Yeah, like that. So how's Karen these days?"

"Good. I lucked out there. Did you ever hear anything else from Lucy?"

Jake lowered his head and looked at his beer.

"Sorry man. You don't have to say anything."

"No, it's okay. I thought she was the one, you know? Like you and Karen. I really thought she'd go to Australia for a few weeks and come back. You know, she'd come running back like in the movies. She just stopped calling me after a few weeks, and she stopped answering my calls."

"That sucks."

"That's not the worst of it. Six weeks to the day after she left, I get a call from her mother inviting me over for dinner. I figure it's a surprise thing and that Lucy's come home. I get over there and her mother tells me that Lucy is breaking up with me. Her mother told me! How cold is that?"

"That's tough. So Karen's making me ask you this. She's got a friend that's pretty hot. Trust me, I got a bruise here," He rolled up his sleeve to show Jake, "Karen bopped me one for looking at this girl the wrong way."

"You're a day late and a loonie short, buddy."

"Oh, sorry. Didn't know you were seeing someone."

"I'm not yet. But there's something there. At least I think there is."

"How'd you meet this girl?"

Jake laughed as he explained.

"She tackled me at the funeral home, thinking I was a crook."

"You could be on to something with this girl. That's the kind of story you end up telling grandchildren someday."

25   Stakeout

The procession of cars slowly looped around the ceremonial circle in the centre of the cemetery. Tammy drove the lead car in the procession. The individual cars edged up to the stopping location of the coach. Lawrence pulled the church truck out of its compartment in the coach and expanded it behind the load door. Tammy released the bier pins holding the casket in place, and Lawrence rolled the casket out of the wagon and maneuvered it onto the church truck. Using laid out plywood, the ensemble was guided to the waiting gravesite. The winds whipped wickedly across the open fields that surrounded and included the graveyard, with little to impede their progress or diminish their force. The mourners cautiously emerged from the vehicles, some anticipating the optimum moment to step out in an attempt to minimize the exposure to the bitter cold. Katrina watched in amazement as the crowd moved in an orchestrated fashion to suddenly become a tightly gathered mass. It was likely the cold that prompted everyone to huddle so closely together.

While she couldn't hear the minister's words from the distance that Jake had strategically positioned his pickup, he was obviously succinct. No sooner had the crowd gelled, than they dissolved into the waiting vehicles. The cars left in a much less procession-like form. Soon the site was deserted, except for Lawrence waiting in the empty coach for the grounds crew to appear so he could get his church truck and take off.

The casket sat solitary on its berth. The flowers that had just minutes earlier been so gently and sadly placed on the top, struggled to hang on. Every few minutes, a single flower would lose the fight to nature and fly off the casket before bouncing across the landscape, the horizontal equivalent to a pebble careening down a rugged cliff.

Katrina broke the silence in the truck.

"Shit, this is boring! They always glamorize this stuff in the movies, like it's thrilling to do this."

Jake glanced over at her and replied "Why do you think we've got this bad rap for eating jelly donuts and drinking coffee? We need them to get through one of these."

Thinking she had a bright idea, Katrina perked up and said "Why don't we play 'I Spy' or something?"

Jake looked at her in disbelief and then sarcastically shot back "Yeah, that'll take long —— I see something that is white — *everything*!"

"Well, it was just a thought," returned a defensive and somewhat embarrassed Katrina, "besides, have *you* got a better idea?"

"As a matter of fact," answered Jake, "let's see what these guys are up to."

"Hey," started Katrina, "I spy with my little eye a WHITE cube van!"

"Very funny," retorted Jake, pulling out a small pair of binoculars.

"So,, where are my binocs at?" questioned Katrina.

"I'm not in the habit of bringing things for my stakeout partners. They're usually quieter too," Jake said with a very slight snarl. "So, who have we got here . . . " Jake wondered out loud.

Two guys lifted the casket off the church truck and oddly placed the casket straddling the open grave. Lawrence folded his now unburdened piece of equipment, stowed it neatly in the designed space in the coach floor, and drove off without saying a word to either of the cemetery workers.

"I'd say the guy on the right is Darth. I recognize the way he walks; he always keeps his hands in his pockets. I feel like he's playing pocket pool when he's near me," finished Katrina.

"A lot of guys stand like that. And I imagine they are playing pocket pool, looking at the likes of you," replied Jake, reversing the snarly attitude of his last comment.

This caught Katrina off guard. She'd been eyeing him over, but she didn't think he had shown the least bit of interest until now. Usually, she can feel a guy's eyes all over her when they're interested, or just acting creepy. But before she could take that discussion any further, Jake continued.

"You're right! It is Darth. He just turned around and sure as shit that's him. That's amazing Katrina!"

She wanted to blurt out 'there's a lot of amazing things about me,' but her shyness once again got the better of her at a crucial moment.

"That other guy is obviously that creep that hangs around Darth all the time . . . what's his name?" asked Jake.

"His brother Hans," responded Katrina, "They're both creeps to me, just different kinds of creeps. It's like these guys belong to some creep organization. I wonder if they pay dues and go to conferences to get the latest creep techniques."

"Sounds like you've studied these types," chuckled Jake as he continued to peer through his binoculars.

"Worse than that," she said with a dejected look and thinking of how she totally misjudged Jonathan. "I seem to always end up dating them."

Jake pulled the binoculars down from his eyes and turned to look at Katrina.

"Well, before you become a card carrying member of the man-hating club, not all of us are like that."

"Unfortunately, the percentage is remarkably high . . . and what makes you so different?" shot Katrina back at him.

Before Jake could come up with examples, out of the corner of his eye he noticed a third man briefly get out of the truck. Neither Jake's binocular enhanced vision, nor Katrina's 'powers' could determine who it was, but it was obvious that he was running the show and that he was not happy. Then, as expected, the two creeps jumped into the grave. The leader looked to be telling them to hurry. He was making frantic gestures with his arms flailing about from behind the van. He never came around to the side where they could get a good look at him. Being in the grave allowed them to get under the casket and undo the screws holding the sides in place. First one slab of ornate wood with brass handles was removed, followed by another, then another until five pieces in total lay on the ground. The creeps clambered out of the hole and hurriedly loaded the goods into the back of the truck, before returning to lower the now pauper-like casket into its permanent resting place.

A fourth guy seemed to materialize right out of the snow. One of the creeps ran over and handed him an envelope, then hustled back to the truck that had already started pulling away from the site. The new guy put his head down slightly and marched into the onrushing wind toward a bobcat that was parked nearby. The machine was then maneuvered into place and the process of filling in the grave commenced.

Katrina started to open her door.

"Where do you think you're going?" barked Jake.

"Lets' go bust that guy – he obviously took a bribe and may know who the leader is!" proclaimed an excited Katrina.

"There's no time for that now," Jake replied, reaching across her to grab the door handle but inadvertently grabbing her breast.

"And there's no time for that now either," a startled Katrina echoed.

"I didn't mean to . . . " stammered Jake, before regaining his composure. "I meant to say that the guy in the bobcat likely doesn't know the leader. Notice that one of the flunkies gave him the money and the leader was in the truck already? We really need to follow the truck *now*, before it gets away. We can come back and question this guy later. I don't imagine there's more than one guy employed here to fill in the holes."

Of course, Jake was right, so Katrina enthusiastically replied "Well, what are you waiting for?"

"You could get your leg back in the truck and close the door," stated Jake, matter of factly.

"Oh," whimpered Katrina, but being slightly flustered she closed the door on her coat. "Sorry," she sheepishly said. She freed the corner of her coat from the door and tried to close it again. This time it caught on her seat belt, which she had forgotten to refasten. Embarrassed, she didn't say anything or even look at Jake. She reopened the door, did up her seat belt, and finally successfully closed the door.

"Done?" laughed Jake.

"Done," confirmed a blushing Katrina.

Fortunately, the truck had to wind around the maze that made up the cemetery roads and hadn't even reached the main road yet. Jake got to within about thirty meters, a nice safe following distance, by the time the truck made it to the main road. The truck barely slowed before it bolted onto the snow-covered route. The winds were now approaching a frenzied pace, making visibility tricky at best. As Jake pulled up to the road, he could barely see in either direction. The openness of the area didn't help. There were no obstacles to slow the onslaught of snow from swirling and building up on the road.

Jake looked back and forth across the road, almost starting out a couple times before stomping on the brake when cars would appear out of the whiteness. He pounded his open hands on the steering wheel. "I can't see a bloody thing!" he proclaimed with exasperation. "I'm afraid we've lost them."

26   *Charity*

Jake and Katrina had time to talk about their next moves while they sat
in the whiteout. Jake came up with a few ideas and they formed a plan.
She would first talk to Darth. She figured he'd either be so nervous that
he'd say nothing (nerd mouth lock around women) or he'd try so hard
to impress her that he'd blabber anything and everything (nervous nerd
core dump). The second part of the plan was to have Jake keep Ben
occupied, questioning him somewhere other than his office. While Jake
was doing that, Katrina would sneak into Ben's office and see if she
could find any papers about the Royal Mahogany caskets. She told Jake
that she'd rather that he did the paper searching, but Jake needed
sufficient reason as a police officer to perform a search. And, of course,
he'd have to deny any involvement if Katrina got caught. Jake tried to
relieve her fears by telling her it was doubtful Ben would have her
arrested if caught.

The next day was another full day at the salon, after which
Katrina arrived at the funeral home. There was quite a crowd tonight.
She was worried that it may prove difficult to find Darth amongst all

the grievers coming and going. She made a quick pass through the working areas of the funeral home, but came up Darth-less. She was hoping he wasn't gone for the day, but she could always catch him tomorrow during the day if so.

Katrina loitered in the entrance for a while in case Darth went by. She elected to kill time by reading the guest books. There were three tables setup in the entrance way, one for each visitation room. On each table sat a guest book and a feathered pen in an imitation inkwell. There was a simple vase with a single yellow rose in each. Beside a short box of Kleenex were a couple of stacks of donation envelopes. A small lockbox was built into each table for the deposit of the envelopes. She supposed that this made people feel better about depositing envelopes with cash inside.

While reading the book in front of a visitation room that had its doors closed for a service, she overheard guests talking at the other tables.

"What do you want me to donate, dear?" a well-dressed, middle-aged man asked his wife, who was wearing a stylish black dress that was perfectly suited for the occasion.

"Just $500, dear. It's not like he was family or anything," the woman answered, obviously thinking this was a paltry sum.

Katrina overheard a few other similar conversations, some with lesser amounts, some with more. She continued watching people slide envelope after envelope into the lock-boxes. These charities must make a fortune in donations, she thought. She had counted ten envelopes deposited in five minutes. If each one had only $100 in it, that added up to $1,000 in five minutes. Again with the math she thought, what's up with all the math? She wondered who the lucky beneficiaries were. She looked down at the envelopes in front of her.

"Heart Stress Foundation" read the one envelope at her table, while the other envelope read "Lungs for Life." She'd never heard of either of them, although their names evoked thoughts of other well-known charities.

She walked over to the second table. Again the envelopes read "Heart Stress Foundation" and "Lungs for Life." She made her way over to the third table - same thing. Odd, she thought. She held up one of each envelope and looked them over.

"Heart Stress Foundation, 99 Chestnut St., Unit 12, Toronto, ON"

"Lungs for Life, 99 Chestnut St., Unit 12, Toronto, ON"

This definitely warranted checking out. But, it would have to wait until later. She needed to talk to Darth first. She decided to make another pass of the backrooms of the funeral home to see if the creep had come out of the woodwork yet. As Katrina walked down the hall toward the back of the building, she almost bumped into Cathy, who emerged from the women's bathroom.

"Hey, Kat! This is getting to be a habit. Love to talk, and talk and talk, but I've got to get back to work. Stewart doesn't like us slacking off on the job. I should finish in about half an hour. I'll look for you then. Toodles."

And without Katrina even getting a word in, Cathy was off and walk-jogging down the hall back to one of the visitation rooms. Katrina was used to Cathy being the talker, but usually she was able to get a few words in between Cathy's amusing stories. They'll be time for that later, she figured. For now, she had to get back to the task at hand - time to track down Darth. This pass around she found him in the employee lounge where she had run into Mr. Smooth Operator earlier.

"Hi, Darth. I don't think we've met yet. I'm Katrina," and she did a little tiny wave closely in front of her chest.

"Yeah, so?"

"I just thought I'd say hi. What's new?"

"Nuttin. You?" Darth looked down toward his leather cowboy boots. He nervously clicked the toes of his boots together as he stood there.

Boy, this is a challenge Katrina thought. So far she's gotten four words out of him. Three were four or less letters, and the other wasn't really a word. She figured she better bring it down a level or two.

"You, know. Stuff. Cuttin' hair. Going to funerals. Going to gravesites . . . say, did I see you out at Mrs. Wilmont's plot yesterday?"

"Don't know. Did ya?"

"Well, it looked like you."

"Couldda been. Why you askin'?" He crossed his arms and straightened his back in a very defensive posture. He was obviously getting agitated.

"Just wonderin'."

"Well, stop wonderin'. Ain't your business." Darth took a quick step toward her, and she almost fell backward. Darth laughed as he brushed by her, barely bumping his arm against her shoulder. "Knew you were the type," and he pulled open the door and exited the room.

That hadn't gone as well as Katrina had hoped. She obviously held no charm over Darth. She couldn't fool him by just trying to talk like him. He seemed like the NASCAR type and probably went for someone a little rougher around the edges — someone who would go toe-to-toe with him if necessary — someone like Cathy. She glanced at her watch. It was close to the time Cathy thought she'd finish. Sure enough, Katrina went out in the hallway and the visitation room was just clearing. She could see Cathy in the crowd, but would have to wait for it to clear a little before approaching her.

After a few minutes Katrina was able to talk to Cathy, who was more than willing to see what she could get out of Darth.

"I'll call you tonight to get the scoop," Katrina told her.

"Not sticking around to hear what I find out?"

"No, I'm supposed to meet Jake about something."

"Who's Jake?" Cathy's eyes lit up as she asked. "You act quickly girl . . . didn't you just dump Jonathan?"

"It's not like that. He's a police officer I'm working with."

"Bull. I can see it in your eyes. You've got the 'hots' for this guy."

"Well, he is kind of cute . . . and muscular. But that's not important right now. We've got something to do for the case."

"Well, I won't get in the way of romance. Let me go see what Darth Nerder has to say. Good luck with your case, as you call it."

Darth stood in the small opening at the back of the funeral home where the stairs to the basement were located. He was looking at some of the items stuck to the bulletin board on the wall. His back was toward Cathy as she moved toward him.

Deciding to take a more direct approach than Katrina, Cathy came right up behind Darth, reached forward, and firmly grabbed his ass.

"Now that's what I'm talking about" Cathy boldly stated to a completely stunned Darth. He hadn't been caught more off guard since he came out of the showers in the ninth grade gym class to find all his clothes disappeared, taken by some grade 12 guys. This was definitely a more pleasant experience but somehow seemed just as awkward to him, especially since he wasn't a big guy and Cathy's butt squeeze was so firm that he fell forward, face first into the bulletin board. As he turned around, Cathy could see that he fell on a couple of push pins and one had nicked his face causing him to have a very slight cut that produced a small trickle of blood.

Cathy was laughing inside at this slight of a man rubbing his face in pain, all the while smearing the drops of blood around. She expected him to say 'Oww . . . what'd you do that for?', but kept on the offensive and decided to not let him respond.

"A tough guy who's not afraid of a little blood?" She purposely hesitated at this point and gave him a look up and down. "Nice boots, cowboy. What do you do around here?"

Darth thought to himself that this was more like the kind of woman that he wanted. Not like that prissy Katrina chick that was fluttering around earlier. He had no use for her type, the kind that likely spends two hours getting ready for anything. He needed a real woman with spunk who wasn't afraid of getting her hands dirty and knew why NASCAR ruled. He gave this new broad a quick once-over and liked what he saw. He wanted desperately to impress her.

"Well, I uh, I do lots of important stuff for the guy who runs this place. I'm like his right-hand man." He nervously looked around, seeing if there was any sign of Ben. BS like this is best spread where there is no one to tell people otherwise.

"Is that so? I'm impressed. What kind of stuff makes you so important, tough guy?"

Darth leaned forward, getting to whispering distance to Cathy.

"I drive the truck on all the special runs from the cemetery."

Cathy put her hand on his waist as they stood closely together. She then leaned in really close to Darth's ear, let go a breath of warm air into it, then whispered back.

"And what could be so special at a cemetery? It's not like you're a bag man for the mob or something."

Darth was overheating with the closeness of Cathy. He could feel her brush up against him in the right areas, and his brain stopped working as his hormones took over.

"Might as well be laundering money. The guy rips off dead people. I can't say much more, but let's just say those expensive caskets don't all make it in the ground. Shit, I probably said too much all ready!" Darth pushed away slightly at realizing he had just blurted out this secret to a relatively complete stranger.

Cathy was relieved by the distance increasing between them. That close to Darth she could tell he'd been working all day and didn't believe in splashing cologne on during the day to keep fresh. She had gotten what she wanted, and used the slight push back as a chance to break away completely.

"So you don't trust me!" Cathy said with a little theatrics as she moved away. "I really thought that we could go someplace. I don't need no 'woosy' guy who can't even say what's on his mind 'cause he's afraid of his boss."

Darth was kicking himself inside. He always blew these things. He tried a pathetic recovery.

"No wait. I was just testing you, to see if you could be trusted." As soon as he said this, he realized that he had just said what she said.

Cathy took a few more steps away, and then turned momentarily to look back and add a little torture to Darth's soul.

"Too bad. Great ass." She shook her head and walked away, leaving Darth pouting like a kid who'd lost his toy Dale Earnhardt car.

27   Ben's Office

Jake entered the funeral home looking for Katrina. He wanted to talk to her before they set their plan in motion for her to search Ben's office. He was careful to stay to the side of the foyer as he entered, trying to avoid visibility from the office. He slipped into the back of one of the visitations rooms and started scanning the small gathering for Katrina. Jake was unaware that at that moment Katrina had finally caught up to Darth. Since he was running about a half hour late, Jake assumed that she'd have long finished talking to Darth.

After a minute of mingling, Jake knew that she was not there. He slid back out the door from which he came and sauntered across the hall to one of the other rooms. The second room was crowded and the service was just about to start. Jake was forced to sit down as everyone else did so. He bobbed his head around in different directions and angles trying to pick Katrina out of the seated crowd. As he was going through this exercise, Katrina had left Darth and was waiting in the foyer for Cathy to free up from the group of people that had suddenly emptied out of the third visitation room. The doors to the room containing Jake had closed only moments before the other visitation room let out, cutting off any chance for either Katrina or Jake to see one another.

Jake had finished his search and had come up empty looking for Katrina in the second visitation room. He continued to sit through the service, not wanting to be disrespectful to the deceased or their family. Katrina, in the meantime, had left talking to Cathy and had returned to the now empty foyer. Without realizing it, she stood just outside Ben's doorway. After looking at her backside for a few moments, Ben called out to her.

"Katrina! So good to see you," he called out as he got up from his desk to greet her. "Why don't you come on in for a few minutes?"

"Oh, hi Ben . . . okay," and she entered his office.

Ben moved only a step or so out from behind his desk before motioning for her to sit down in one of his large comfy leather chairs.

"So, how have things been going?" and without giving her a chance to reply he continued. "I've been getting good feedback from our clients about your work."

"Good. I'm glad," Katrina replied, glancing first at her watch, then toward the door for a sign of Jake.

"Got a date?" Ben asked, noticing Katrina inspecting her watch.

"Oh. Sorry. My mind's just on something else."

"Never mind. By the way," he paused while he looked around the surface of his desk, "I've got a check for you somewhere here - for the first few jobs you did."

"Thanks. I can put it to good use."

Ben's searching had progressed from eyeballing his desk top to starting to move papers around. "I know it's here somewhere . . . "

Before he could finish his sentence or his search, a loud knocking came from the doorway and Jake stuck his head in.

"Hope I'm not intruding . . . "

"No, not at all" Ben replied. "I was just trying to find this young lady her paycheque."

"I was wondering if you could spare a few minutes to discuss the case with me," Jake said as he edged the rest of his body into the room.

"No problem. Why don't you come in?"

Of course, Jake didn't want to meet in the office per their plan. And since Katrina was already there, she wouldn't have to sneak in.

"I think we should discuss in private," he replied, looking at Katrina as he said it. He turned to Katrina. "No offence, Miss. You can stay put. We'll just step out into another room for a few minutes."

"None taken," Katrina replied, partly grinning.

"All right. Excuse me, Katrina. I'll come back in a few minutes and we'll find that paycheque." Jake followed Ben toward the selection room, which was full of sample caskets and urns.

Katrina wasn't exactly sure what she was looking for. Jake hadn't found any markings on the casket indicating who made the fake casings. She went over to the door quickly to make sure the coast was clear. Ben and Jake were partly down the hallway that led to the back of the funeral home. She wasn't sure where to look, or what she was looking for beside something with the style name of Royal Mahogany on it. Ben's desk was a good place to start. Although the drawers had locks, none of them were locked. Ben probably wasn't expecting to leave suddenly like he did. She rummaged through one side, finding folders full only with brochures and the like. She moved to the other side and pulled open the large bottom drawer. This looked promising. There hung a number of file folders, neatly labeled and filled with papers. The folder tabs contained names of suppliers that the funeral home used. She remembered overhearing the phone conversation the prior week and finally realized what Ben was complaining about when he needed 'another set' right away. He likely had a need for more than one at a time. What was the name on the side of that truck she saw in the lot the one day? She flipped through the tabs until spotting one that triggered her memory – Stan's Custom Craft Woodworking. She pried the file open wider with her fingers, not wanting to pull it completely out because she knew she didn't have much time. There were two pages only in the file. Both for the same amount and both invoices simply said "Made to order mahogany woodworking." All the other files were bursting with multiple pages that indicated a lot of activity with each supplier. She was just closing the desk drawer when she was startled by a woman's voice.

"What are you doing?" It was Tammy. She was under the door jam, so she likely hadn't been there long.

Katrina was a little flustered, but somehow contrary to usual performance, regained her composure quickly.

"Oh, hi, Tammy. I was just looking for my paycheque. Ben was trying to find it and stepped out. I figured it was on his desk somewhere. Just then she happened to spot it on the floor by the corner of his desk. "Got it!" she exclaimed with relief as she bent down and plucked it off the carpet.

"Sorry," Tammy apologized "but I thought you were snooping around or something. Guess I'm still not very trusting after that creep boyfriend of mine."

"Don't worry about it."

Just then Ben came back in the room.

Katrina walked toward Ben, waving her cheque in the air. "Found it! I'll see you two tomorrow. I'm beat. Goodnight."

28 *Charity by Any Other Name*

The morning at Kat's Kuts was a busy one, mostly regulars getting perms and colouring done to make the natural colour of their roots disappear. There were a few walk-ins thrown in for good measure. Katrina found just a few minutes to update Marlene with the latest news. Katrina was anxious to skip out at lunch and check out the charity office on Chestnut. Marlene's enthusiasm for sleuthing had rubbed off on her, as Katrina had now found herself trying to figure out a collection of things going on down at Shady Rest. First it was stolen watches and jewelry, followed by the casket scam, and now she was digging into some suspicious sounding charities. How could so much illegal behaviour happen in one small funeral home? Were any of these things connected? She hadn't caught up with Cathy yet to find out what information was pried out of Darth. Nor had Katrina talked to Jake about what she saw in Ben's drawers – she better make sure she doesn't quite word it like that! That brings up Mr. Smooth Operator, another shady character (and a bad pun).

Katrina left work shortly after 1:00 P.M., deciding she'd grab a bite to eat somewhere later. She had checked the appointment book for the afternoon and it wasn't anything that Kevin and Marlene couldn't handle. She headed out to catch the subway downtown, as Chestnut was down by the U of T. She had a niece stay last year at a residence on Chestnut. It was a former hotel converted into residences. Very spacious apartments for students, she thought at the time. Her niece had since moved out to a small apartment with a couple of friends made during the year. The new digs were nothing in comparison but left a lot more money in their pockets. Actually the money went back into their parent's pockets, at least in concept anyways. The kids, of course, squeezed it back out, supposedly for food and clothing, but much of it ended up as entertainment expenses.

Katrina was trying to visualize which building would house the charities based on the address and from what she could recall in her mind of the layout of the street. She assumed it was the building next to the residence. It had some street level stores like a laundry mat, convenience store, a 24x7 pizza franchise, and dry cleaners. There were a few others, but she couldn't remember. Katrina thought there were apartments above the stores. As she walked past the string of small stores she came to a set of double doors with 99 Chestnut painted on the semi- circle window overtop the doors. Inside the doors there was a directory showing a list of offices on the second and third floors. Apartments seemed to occupy floors four and up. She looked again at the listing on the wall and this time started with her finger at the top and slowly went down the list until she came to the H's and found 'Heart

Stress Foundation', and then 'Lungs for Life' shortly after. Unit 12 was located on the second floor. Katrina felt it was safe to take the stairs in this building and headed on up. She exited the stairwell and looked for some sign of which direction to turn for unit 12 but found none. She lately turned left in these cases, figuring that she would normally go right, and she was normally wrong. It seemed to work out and so she didn't care if it made a whole lot of sense.

She had gone only about 15 feet when she heard a British accent quite clearly coming from the office ahead.

"It's all quite reputable, I assure you. We British pride ourselves at being above board, you know." Then there was a pause, as this discussion was apparently over the phone. Then he continued, "Brilliant. I'll see you here at 4:00 P.M. sharp! Look forward to meeting you in person, Miss Emily."

Katrina was fairly certain she recognized the voice as she approached the door. 'Stewart!' she blurted out to herself. Sure enough, there was the sign on the wall beside the door:

Heart Stress Foundation

Lungs for Life

Friends of the Deceased

S. Windle, CEO

Stewart Windle! She knew about the Friends of the Deceased gig, and was actually somewhat impressed that Stewart had come up with such a clever idea. His Life of the Party scheme was also well-conceived, even if poorly executed and eventually led to a major fiasco. That fiasco, though, had led to Katrina getting the seed money for her business. Stewart had pointed her to his stash of money in his haste to escape with his life. She often wondered if Stewart had any idea how much was under that rug or if he thought it was only a few hundred dollars. Should she tell him?

Katrina had mixed feelings about Stewart Windle. She was very grateful for the money, of course. Stewart did have the manners of a true gentleman, a quality that Katrina wished a few more guys possessed. He was an impeccable dresser and very neat. He didn't appear to have any truly distasteful habits that she had noticed. And while she didn't see it in the least, Cathy thought he was kind of cute.

All that said, there was always something that felt a little crooked about dealing with Stewart. Maybe it was the 90 percent fake British accent (giving him some credit for his early years in Britain before moving to Canada), and the accompanying pompous attitude that contributed to her concerns — she never liked snobs who talked down to people — it seemed un-Canadian to her. Perhaps it was simply that his name looked like swindle. Regardless, she was going to confront him about the charities. She was convinced that there must be something shifty about it if Stewart was involved.

She reached for the door knob to open it, but then thought better of barging in and decided she should knock first and did so.

"Enter," beckoned Stewart's voice. As Katrina entered and Stewart saw who it was, he stood up and held his arms open to greet her like they were long lost best friends. "Katrina, my dear, how absolutely delightful to see you again!"

Katrina held out her hand to shake. She wasn't much on the whole hugging strangers thing – the closeness to someone she didn't feel comfortable around kind of gave her the willies. She wanted to avoid any physical contact with Stewart and thought a handshake was a good alternative. Stewart extended his hand to shake. Once he had a grip on her hand, he pulled her firmly toward him and gave her the embrace that she dreaded. His arms wrapped around her as she froze, arms straight down at her sides. Her head pulled back and she looked away from him like she was trying to catch her breath. After a few seconds in this helpless pose, she was able to lift her hands up to his chest and gently push herself away.

"Nice to see you too, Stewart," she said, brushing herself off like she may have caught his dishonesty.

"What brings you down here? Cathy's not here."

"Cathy's what? No, I came to see about these charities. I've noticed them at all of the funeral services at Shady Rest and it seemed suspicious that every funeral had the same charities."

"Totally legitimate my dear, registered with the government and all that rot."

"But does any of the money go to real charity work?"

"Katrina! You imply that I am somehow dishonest. I am saddened that you should think this."

"So, does any of the money go to real charity work?" she reiterated, used to Stewart's evasive techniques from dealing with him before.

"Yes, some does."

"What do you mean by 'some'?"

"I have administrative overhead you know."

Katrina looked around the office— a desk, a chair, a phone, an old copier. The corner of the office had boxes from Super Quick Copy – likely the donation envelopes. No assistants in site.

"Yes, I can see you have a lot of expenses to run this place."

"I meet the minimum allowable requirements and make donations to hospitals, foundations, etc. for research and whatever it is they do. And I have some extra expenses that you don't see here."

"You mean like paying to put your donation envelopes out whenever possible."

"I've said enough already I'm sure."

"That's okay. You don't need to tell me anything more. I'm helping out with a related police investigation, so they'll be interested to hear from me about this racket too. They may even think you're linked to the jewelry thefts and the casket changing scam happening down there."

"Now hold on a minute. A gentleman such as me would never lower his standards to resort to petty theft of jewelry. And casket changing sounds like it involves manual labour, and I simply do not do manual labour. I don't even like to supervise manual labour!"

"But still, the police would be interested in what happened in Montreal . . . "

"So the squeaky clean Katrina has stooped to blackmail, has she?"

"I just need you to do a couple of background checks for me on people at Shady Rest."

"Why can't your police friend do that?"

She wondered how he knew so much about what she's been involved in lately. She pressed on knowing he had many connections.

"Because I know you'll get the real scoop from your network of friends. And as payment I won't say anything about your 'for profit' charities that you're working here."

Stewart chuckled to himself. "I'd say that you've found me the proper motivation to begin my search."

29 *The Magic of Charity*

Stewart Windle was surprised to see Katrina appear in his office. He was part surprised and part tickled that she would step out of character and attempt to blackmail him. It was a funny twist he thought – sweet Katrina gone bad, and him walking the straight and narrow.

Far from the impression that he gave Katrina, he didn't feel overly threatened by her talk of exposing his Montreal racket to his father. Here's that Boris creep coming back to haunt him again! It was obvious that Katrina's ex-roommate had spilled the beans, but surely she had no details to back up Boris' claims. Whatever, Stewart figured. He'd help out Katrina regardless and convinced himself that it wasn't her great body, stunning looks, or mesmerizing green eyes that made him agree. Stewart looked at it as just another act of charity.

When he started his charitable foundations, Stewart figured it was an easy and legal way to subsidize his Friends of the Deceased venture, or, perhaps the other way around. Either way, he knew it was best to have more than one hand in play. Just like in poker, you have to read the other players, their bets, the cards on the table, and realistically be able to assess your own situation in light of the first three. Having two businesses gave him flexibility to move money from one play to the other if needed.

A few months after kicking off the charities, Stewart started putting the minimum legal amount on cheques and presenting them to research centres. Initially, he got phone hang ups by a few people who thought he was messing with them – maybe it was the British accent. Once people found out that he really was giving money to organizations, Stewart got courted via sales pitches, tours, and the occasional free drink. Once he sized them up and their potential to recognize his charity's contribution publicly, he would agree to donate. This led to invitations to galas to present oversized cheques. He loved galas. Any day he got to wear a tuxedo was a good day.

This is where Stewart learned the true magic of charity. Giving leads to getting back in return, and often at an exponential rate of return. He had decent connections already from his childhood buddies, and occasionally leveraging the family name when it suited him. But the contacts that he made at the galas opened so many new doors that he had to buy a second Rolodex and hire more staff for Friends of the Deceased. In turn, he increased the percentage of the collected money that actually went to charities well above the minimum amount, which increased the frequency of the donations, the number of galas, the list of new contacts and, most importantly, the number of new clients. It was the proverbial snowball rolling downhill.

The other huge benefit of the charity work was the benevolent image Stewart garnered, not only in the community, but also more importantly with his parents – obviously his new reputation hadn't made it all the way to Katrina's corner of the city. Stewart finally felt that his father's hand had come off of the cord holding the trust-fund plug. The whole going straight thing was actually working out for him.

So when Katrina tried her little blackmail stunt, Stewart could have easily dismissed her. But he had a feeling that charity extended beyond giving away money, so helping her would be his latest act of charity. He didn't know how it would pay him back, but that was half the fun of the concept – the payback often came in unusual or unexpected ways. Stewart decided to play along with Katrina's blackmail attempt for fun.

Now, it was time to utilize those burgeoning Rolodexes of his to get this desperate girl her tidbits of information.

30 *Gossip*

"So Katrina, I feel like you've been ignoring me lately," were the first words in the morning from a slightly whiny Kevin as Katrina entered the salon.

"Good morning to you too, Kevin."

"Don't be changing the subject," he replied.

"Sorry. Let me get my coat off and we'll catch up with a cup of coffee."

"Now you're talking honey," and he went off to fetch a couple cups of fresh coffee. It wasn't as good as a Tim's coffee but was better than most he'd had in his years of hairdressing. He'd managed to talk Katrina into spending a few extra bucks on Java to keep him happy, although he needed to perform only a half-princess routine to convince her. He was willing to go the full-princess routine for good coffee if necessary.

"So, where do I start?" she said somewhat rhetorically. "There has been so much going on . . . " Katrina words were stopped by Marlene entering the salon.

"Looks like some gossip is about to happen," Marlene said, noting the two chairs closely facing each other and the two cups of coffee on the small table between. "Hold up a few minutes girls. I want to get in on this." She ran to the back to hang up her coat and quickly pour a cup of coffee before pulling up a chair.

About 20 minutes and 20 questions later, Katrina got to the end of her recap.

"Well, I for one am certainly glad that I didn't get involved in all these shenanigans," Kevin concluded as he stood up from his chair.

"And I want to get more involved now!" the energetic Marlene responded, getting a look from Kevin like she was sucking up to Katrina. Noticing 'the look', Marlene continued "You know I like the sleuthing Kat . . . tell Cat Woman over there before he claws my eyes out."

"Yes, I know Marlene. Kevin, behave. Marlene isn't brown nosing *this* time."

"That's better," and Kevin walked over to his station and finished preparing it for the day. Marlene at first looked insulted, then realized that Katrina had done it to pacify Kevin, so she let it slide.

The morning was fairly slow, giving Katrina time to think about different whodunit scenarios. It seemed like every time she chased a lead on one crime, a new crime was uncovered. She still hadn't solved the first one and felt that she should refocus on that one. After all, she started looking into it as a tribute to Duncan, and to try and recover his stolen watch. Somehow stealing from the dead seemed really low to Katrina. She had suffered through many old cowboy movies that her

Dad made her watch when she was young. She never thought it right when they took the good cowboy boots off the dead guy because "Tex ain't got no use for these now, and he just done bought them."

For some reason, Katrina felt disappointed that Stewart was involved in the charity scheme, although he likely was within the lines of the law – at least barely. Cathy had talked so highly of Stewart that she was beginning to think he had turned a new leaf. Maybe Cathy didn't know about the charity thing, or maybe she was part of it? No, that's not like Cathy – get that thought out of your mind she told herself. It probably wasn't like Stewart to share the profits with anyone unless he had to. Some people would call that cheap, but as the British and Katrina's mother would say, 'he was thrifty'.

Katrina had finished storing a new order of shampoo and conditioner in the backroom, and as she returned to the front of the salon she was startled to see Stewart standing there.

"Well, I suppose the masses have to go somewhere to get their locks trimmed." He looked around the place, with his nose somewhat curled up showing his general distaste with the place.

"What are you doing here, Stewart?"

"You did ask me to find out some information for you."

"But you've had only a few hours this morning."

"My dear, if you want to keep from a life as a labourer, you have to develop other skills. And I am very skilled at finding out information. The name of the game in my line of work is connections, and I, my dear, am full of them."

"I can tell just by listening to you talk that you're full of it," came the quip from Kevin.

Marlene and Katrina giggled in agreement.

"So, what did you find out?" Katrina asked, still smiling.

"Not so fast. I think I would be more inclined to tell you while you give me a courtesy trim."

"Speaking of trim," Kevin began, but stopped when he saw Katrina give him the 'zip it' look. No doubt Kevin was going to make some remark about the few extra pounds that Stewart carried on his frame.

Stewart ignored the partial remark and lowered himself into Katrina's chair. She covered him up with a cape and fastened the Velcro at the back.

"Razor or clippers?"

"Clippers, of course. Razor – how lower class indeed."

"So, what did you find out?" as she began snipping away at the hair on the back of his neck.

"The assistant, Tammy Parker, had some major financial issues. She's fighting her way back from them pretty well. She was in a failed business. Word is her partner took most of her clients, and left her with a pile of debts."

"That's what she told me too. I don't think she's crooked though."

"I concur. Otherwise I wouldn't partner with her to distribute my envelopes."

"Tammy's involved with your scam? I must have read her wrong!"

"It's not a scam, my dear. It's completely legit. I told you that before. There's nothing illegal about it."

"And that's supposed to convince me that she's not crooked?"

"You still don't trust me, do you? Tammy gets a small percentage as an administrative fee. It's added up nicely for her and it looks like she's putting it right down on her debt."

"So, what about Ben?"

"He's also in financial trouble. But he seems to be stuck there. I'm told that he had some major omissions in his stated income. Our friends at the Canada Revenue Agency haven't looked too kindly upon it. He owes some major back taxes."

"What do you consider major?"

"Close to a quarter million, from what I hear."

"That's pretty major."

"Yes, my dear it is. Ben seems to have surrounded himself with some real stellar workers too. Tammy's the only one that has a legitimate background. The other cast of characters all seem to have some type of criminal record."

"Like what are we talking, record wise?"

"Well, the driver has a rap sheet that includes burglary, assault, and indecent exposure."

"I don't think I want to know . . . "

"Well, my dear, you're going to. He got all liquored up at a Leafs game one night and obviously delirious over a rare victory, ran nude down Yonge Street."

"Oh that's pretty sad."

"Worse yet, he was running, winky in hand yelling 'Let me introduce you to my little friend . . . Lawrence Junior."

"That guy's got class written all over him."

"Class dimwit, perhaps. And Darth is a real gem too. He got caught five times stealing purses from old ladies. Three times the old ladies themselves tripped him up before he got away. Once he stole the purse and ran right into an oncoming car. The other time he ran into an oncoming bike currier. Can you say loser?"

"Done."

"Yes, that's about it."

"No, I mean your trim is done."

"Right." Stewart looked at his watch, a Rolex of course. "Perfect timing. Cathy should get back any minute now."

"Cathy? Back?"

"Yes. She dropped me off and we're going out for lunch."

"To discuss her next Friends of the Deceased gig, I suppose?"

"No, it's a social lunch. She didn't tell you did she . . . "

"Tell me what?"

"Cathy and I are living together, my dear."

31 *Pub and Grub*

It was the end of another day of work, and Katrina was still feeling put out that Cathy hadn't told her about dating Stewart, let alone living with him. At first Katrina felt anger that Cathy hadn't told her. Moving in with someone was a major step that friends would talk about. Thinking about it made her feel more mad and disappointed, like Cathy didn't trust her. The more she thought about it, she recalled a couple of conversations and realized that Cathy had probably tried to tell her but Katrina cut her off. She felt like having a beer, or two. She didn't have to ask twice to get Marlene to go with her, as Marlene wanted to get back into the crime-solving game after their chat early in the day. Kevin had plans with the hubby, so he declined the invite, then followed by making a remark about being grateful that he wouldn't have to listen to Marlene suck up to Katrina.

Katrina didn't waste much time finding a bar to drink at, heading straight across the street to the Pub and Grub. The food was greasy and fatty and was palatable really only after you were too drunk to care and wanted something in your system solely to fight the morning hangover. The beer, however, was always cold, and Katrina could always sweet talk Jason the bartender into reaching into the back of the freezer to get her an ice cold frosted mug.

The Pub and Grub was a typical roadhouse, except that it wasn't situated in the 'burbs like most. After ordering their beers at the bar, to get the frosted mugs and to get their pints quickly, the girls settled in at a booth along the side of the building. There were no windows along that side and it was a little darker than the rest of the place, but Katrina wanted someplace more private than the tables scattered throughout the middle of the bar. For one, she wanted to scheme with Marlene and when the two of them sat at the tables, it was a steady procession of guys trying their lines on one or both of them in hopes of getting lucky. Of course, they got a lot of free beer that way, but today wasn't about the beer – at least not totally.

"So, I want you to help me catch the jewel thief," Katrina said as she finished a long sip of cold beer.

"I'm all ears!" replied Marlene, not having touched her beer yet, but nervously wiping at the frosting on the outside of the mug. She then took a quick, small sip as she listened.

"I'm sure that it's Lawrence the driver that's stealing the watches and other jewelry. I thought of doing this myself, but getting close to him kind of creeps me out."

"Thanks, I think."

"I want you to convince him that you've got a side business of flipping stolen watches out of the salon. Get him to commit to a delivery at the funeral home and I'll be there with Jake to bust him."

"Oh, shit! I forgot to tell you. Jake called looking for you just before we left. You were in the bathroom so I told him to meet you here."

"Good thing you're not an administrative assistant. What time did he say he'd get here?" Katrina looked at her watch as she asked.

"Now."

"Hey, ladies. Did you save any beer for me?"

Katrina was startled by his sudden appearance and bumped the table in the booth, shaking everything quite violently. Both girls managed to grab their beers before they could spill. Katrina was thankful now that they weren't at a table, for it likely would have tipped with the force she bumped the bolted down booth table. She was flustered as much by Jake's unannounced arrival as she was pissed off at Marlene for not telling her and giving her time to freshen up. She was sure that her hands still smelled like a funky combination of shampoo, conditioner, and gel. Her clothes likely smelled like the chemicals used for doing perms - not her idea of how to impress Jake, especially as he cozied up beside her in the booth.

"Hi, Jake. We were just going over the case and I was telling Marlene of my plan to nab Lawrence."

"You should leave the police work to me."

"Too late now, you already got me involved. And now we need Marlene's help too."

"Great, more paperwork. Tell me your plan, and I'll tell you if I think it will work."

Katrina explained her plan to Jake, and he was pleasantly surprised at how much thought she had put into it. She even had thought of signals they could use for certain things and some contingency plans in case the plan went wrong. Earlier in the day, her plan had Marlene asking Lawrence if he could come up with a gold necklace encrusted in diamonds, like the one for Mrs. Wilmont's reward. But then she thought maybe a watch would be more like something Marlene could sell out of the salon. Katrina wanted to amaze Jake with her plan so she was very careful to consider the details.

"I have to say that I'm impressed. You must watch a lot of police movies. I've got a couple little changes but overall, nice job."

Katrina was blushing at his appraisal of her plan. She was used to guys drooling over her for her looks and found his appreciation for her thinking as exciting and even turning her on. She was a short time out of a relationship and didn't want to jump right back into one, but what was there not to like about this guy? Katrina just didn't know if he thought the same way. She thought his eyes were telling him that he did.

"Is it getting warm in here?" Katrina asked, the closeness of Jake affecting her body temperature.

"It's my fault. I just turned up the candle," Marlene teased her.

"So, let me tell you about my plan for the casket scheme," said Jake.

"Who do you think it is?" asked Marlene.

"I'm not positive, as both Ben and Tammy have motive and access to commit the crime. I'm leaning toward Ben, but my plan involves both of them, and that guy Darth that Katrina's friend talked to at Shady Rest. What was her name again?"

"Cathy," they both chimed in at the same time.

"Yes. That's it, Cathy. Anyway, I've done some homework and there's a visitation tomorrow for someone with the last name Ramirez that's getting the Royal Mahogany casket. I've also heard that they've hired FREDs, so I'm hoping your friend Cathy is there." Jake proceeded to lay out his plan to the girls, who quietly sat and finished their first round of beer and started their second that arrived with Jake's pint of stout. Finally something about him that Katrina didn't approve of – she didn't know how anybody drank that room temperature crap. She tried drinking it from a frosted mug one time and, besides the odd looks from the bartender when she requested it, she still found the taste appalling. But if that was the worst thing about Jake, she'd manage.

Marlene couldn't contain her excitement about the plans.

"It would be great to solve this case and bust some crooks! And that reward money would certainly help you out Katrina."

Jake leaned back from the table, looking confused.

"There's no reward money."

"Yes there is." Marlene replied. "The daughter of Mrs. Wilmont offered Katrina $5,000 to recover her stolen jewels. That will help with the salon debts!"

There could have been steam coming from Jake's ears.

"You should have told me about this Katrina."

"What does it matter? We need to catch the bad guys anyway. If we're lucky and we recover Mrs. Wilmont's jewelry, I get a reward."

"That's not the point. The problem is that the police don't work with private detectives because their motivation is usually to recover property, not to solve the crime or make sure that our bust sticks. They are in it for the money and it often jeopardizes our police investigation."

"I'm sorry, I didn't think . . . "

Jake didn't say another word. He took a twenty out of his wallet to cover his bill and got up and left.

Marlene apologized to Katrina.

"I'm sorry, I didn't think . . . "

"That makes two of us, apparently."

32   *Junk in my Truck*

The next evening couldn't come soon enough for Katrina. In spite of not sleeping well, having tossed and turned a good portion of the night thinking about pissing off Jake, she felt pretty good. Likely running a little on adrenalin she thought, but she was ready to go. In spite of his concerns last night, Jake was picking her and Marlene up after work and taking them down to the funeral home.

The two of them were waiting by the door when Jake pulled up in his pickup truck. Marlene stepped outside while Katrina turned off most of the lights, set the alarm, and locked up the salon. Jake, in the meantime, had gotten out of his truck and waited for Katrina.

"Marlene. Can I have a minute with Katrina?" Jake politely asked.

"Okay. I'll just make sure Katrina locked up."

Jake walked over to Katrina, put his hand on her shoulder, and guided her away from the door and Marlene's earshot.

"Look, I just want to say I'm sorry. I overreacted last night."

"No, it's okay. I messed up accepting the reward offer."

"That's the point. How would you know? You aren't a real private investigator. You shouldn't be expected to know the rules. I'm sure your intentions are good. So, can we just forget it ever happened? Do you accept my apology?"

"I do, but only if you accept mine for causing you any trouble."

"Deal. Ready to go?" Jake extended his arm to escort her to the truck. He waved over to Marlene and she grabbed his other arm. As they neared the truck, Jake released Marlene's arm. He opened the door, gallantly bowed slightly, and motioned for Marlene to step up into the truck. Marlene took a small step toward the door and looked inside. The back seat was buried in all kinds of stuff, none of which was going anywhere. That meant that all three of them would sit up front. She stopped in her tracks and pretended to fumble through her purse for a minute.

As Katrina stepped closer, Marlene put a glove on her back and pushed her toward the door, ensuring that Katrina would sit next to Jake in this cozy seating arrangement. Katrina looked back and gave Marlene a look, like 'what was that for'. Marlene followed her into the cab of the truck and Jake closed the door behind her before jogging around the front of the truck to his side.

Jake settled into his seat and fastened his shoulder belt, brushing up against Katrina in the process.

"Buckle up, ladies. I'd hate to have to give you tickets for not wearing your seat belts."

Katrina flashed back to the stripper cop she hired for Kevin, imaging Jake in the outfit and cuffing her.

The girls jostled around, trying to retrieve their seat belts from between the seat and back, and Katrina couldn't help but bump against Jake a few times as she did. It was tight quarters indeed, as Katrina's side was fully up against Jake and all she could smell was his scent. Katrina looked at Marlene and mouthed 'Thank you."

Marlene looked at the clutter in the back seat as they pulled away from the curb.

"I hear that you can tell a lot about a man by what he keeps in his truck."

"It's just a bunch of stuff. Sorry about the mess. Otherwise we wouldn't have to crowd in here like this." Jake apologized, although he was enjoying being so close to Katrina.

"I'm fine. I think it's quite comfy," Katrina responded, trying to make no big deal about the squeeze.

"So, let's see what he's got, so to speak. Work boots, covered in mud. Quite big. What are those? 12's?"

"13's"

"Nice," Marlene smiled as she replied, nudging Katrina in the arm. "Four orange pylons," she continued with the inventory.

"For emergencies, to mark off hazards."

"Two hockey sticks."

"Gear is airing out at home."

"Thank you for that! Is that a skateboard?"

"From an undercover gig a while back."

"Is that your laundry in that blue duffle bag?"

"No. It's some clothes from my brother's kids that I'm supposed to drop off at the church downtown."

"Good. Check off gives back to the community on your list Katrina."

"What list?" both Katrina and Jake replied.

"Just kidding. What else have we got back there . . . an old blanket, a small roadside kit maybe . . . ?"

"Yep. Jumper cables, flares, you know."

"And what's that hiding under the blanket?" and she elbowed Katrina while trying to reach over the seat to investigate. "Did a lady friend forget her purse and heels?"

Jake was blushing.

Katrina looked disappointed.

Then Marlene pulled the black shoes over Katrina's head and into the front seat.

"You must like your women large . . . and I mean very large," and she held up the largest pair of women's shoes either of the girls had ever seen.

Jake kept blushing.

Katrina's look changed from disappointment to disgust.

"All right. It's from an undercover assignment I'd rather not talk about."

"I hope it didn't involve getting under the covers. The guy would have been in for a hell of a surprise," Marlene teased him.

Katrina looked relieved.

"Thank God we are here!" Jake announced with relief. He took a lot of ribbing for a couple of weeks after that job. He was glad that all the other detectives had finally stopped calling him Jackie and whistling at him.

"But we're not at the funeral home yet?" Katrina said, slightly puzzled.

"No, but we're at the bus stop where you get off at. I don't want our suspects at the funeral home to know we are working together. Sorry about making you walk."

Marlene couldn't resist. "Maybe we can borrow those nice heels of yours."

33 *To Catch a Thief*

Jake had done some questioning around the funeral home. He was careful to avoid having Lawrence connecting the girls to him. They didn't hide the connection between the girls, but they did want Marlene to come off as working the black market watch gig behind Katrina's back.

Jake planned to get both Ben and Tammy together in the Ramirez visitation room, and not in the office. This required that he find them individually and set appointments to meet him in the visitation room fifteen minutes before the service. He'd rendezvous with Katrina and they'd listen in on Marlene's rendezvous with Lawrence. Jake had already put a small wire on Marlene so they could hear her conversation. Jake arrived first and went to set up his meeting. After their short walk from the bus stop, Katrina went to find Cathy to fill her in on what was going on and get her to play along as needed. Marlene went to the restroom to freshen up.

In the restroom, Marlene touched up her makeup and sprayed on an excess of perfume. From all accounts, an overdose of perfume was likely the right touch for Mr. Smooth Operator. She also adjusted her blouse to reveal more for Lawrence's leering eyes. A few more minutes poofing out her hair and she'd be ready.

Jake, in the meantime, had easily found Ben in his office and arranged the meeting time and place. Ben seemed curious as to why they couldn't talk right then and there. Jake explained that he had to call into the office first, so they'd have to meet later. Ben seemed to buy it and went back to his paperwork. Next, Jake took a cruise through the visitation rooms before he found Tammy talking in the hallway to Darth. This seemed suspicious to Jake, but then his job required him to be suspicious of everyone and everything. Darth looked menacingly at Jake as he went by, as least as menacingly as Darth was capable of, which rated somewhere around two on a scale of ten.

Katrina hadn't located Cathy so much as Cathy had found her.

"I'm so sorry Katrina. Stewart told me how surprised you were about me living with him. I hadn't told him that I didn't tell you. You know I tried to tell you about Stewart . . . "

"I know Cathy. I'm sorry for not listening. It's just all this other stuff on my mind."

The two hugged to confirm the apology.

"I know what's on your mind. I saw Jake walking around a few minutes ago. That'd keep my mind busy too . . . not to mention my body!"

"Enough! But speaking of Jake, I wanted to tell you our plans for today. You might be able to help."

"Sure, anything for you, Kat. But for today you need to call me Ramona."

Katrina filled in Cathy, explaining the possible need for a diversion at some point during the Ramirez visitation. Cathy ensured Katrina that it would be her pleasure to draw the attention of the entire room to her when called upon. She already had something in mind, based on the profile that Stewart had given her for Ramona.

Jake had gone back out to the truck, where Katrina was to meet him for taping Marlene's conversation with Lawrence. He was a minute or two early, so he wasn't even thinking that he had missed her. After a few more minutes passed, he did worry that something had gone wrong. His first impression of Katrina was that she was a dumb blonde bombshell. He recalled the way she was all over him in the visitation room the first time they met. But after hearing her well thought out plan, and getting to know her a bit more, he realized that there was much more to this lady than just her surface beauty. Although the beauty certainly didn't hurt, it was nice to meet someone who he could talk to while looking at. There was a certain naivety to her that he initially mistook for lack of intelligence, but he had grown accustomed to her quirkiness and actually enjoyed seeing that side of her come out every so often.

"Sorry I'm late," she said looking at her watch as she closed the door behind her, once again getting her coat caught in it.

"At least you're consistent," Jake laughed as she opened the door long enough to free the trapped tail of her coat.

"You didn't miss anything yet. Is Marlene reliable?" and before he could finish he heard a voice over the wire.

"I just saw Lawrence head into the lunch room and I'm following. Wish me luck," and you could hear her opening the door.

"That guy must spend all of his time in there!"

"Shhh. I want to hear this in case I need to go in and get her out."

Marlene proceeded into the lunch room and saw Lawrence sitting at a table, reading the *Toronto Sun*, or at least looking at the pictures.

"Lawrence, I presume?"

"Who's asking, beautiful?"

Marlene turned and pushed the door shut, then faced Lawrence again.

"I hear that you're the man to hook me up."

"Are you looking for stud services, because I'd have no problem performing those for you?" He tilted his sunglasses down and looked over them to ogle her. He stared at her for a while before returning his eyes up to her face.

"I usually don't mix work and pleasure, but rules are made to be broken. My connection was right; you do look like a combination of a young Robert Goulet and James Bond." She knew that Katrina would get a kick out of overhearing that line. "I'm looking for a supplier for some high-end watches. Not replicas or knock-offs, but the authentic stuff."

"What does a hot little number like you need with expensive watches?"

"I work in a hair salon and I've got a nice little market established. Cutting hair doesn't pay a lot, if you didn't guess, and I'm a girl who likes the finer things in life. Lifestyle takes money."

"So, assuming I could, why would I help you?"

"My supplier became unreliable and I couldn't trust him anymore. I've got some orders backed up that I need filled ASAP. As a result, I'm looking to pay top dollar for my first delivery. I'm also assuming you could use a good steady way to get rid of your acquired goods in the future. It's a win-win for both of us."

"So, how many are you looking for right now, and how many more later?"

"I need five today. And one must be a Movado, Black Quartz." Jake had checked Mr. Ramirez yesterday and fed this information to Marlene at the Pub and Grub. She leaned over the table as she said this, exposing a tease of cleavage for Lawrence to think about and a strong dose of perfume to stimulate him. She figured this weasel might need a little extra motivation, and it worked.

"Sure. I can do that. Movado Black Quartz, eh? I don't have one in stock, but think I know where to get one today."

"Good. I like doing business in very public places. Meet me in one hour in whichever visitation room is full," she finished, knowing very well the Ramirez room would be packed at that time.

"And maybe after that . . . ," Lawrence put his hand on his belt buckle and moved it up and down with his thumb, "we can play Cat in the Hat Long Division."

Marlene shuttered to think of the line of crap that she was about to hear, but felt compelled to go along.

"Oh, how do you play that?"

"Well dear, you'll be Thing 1 and I'll be Thing 2. Then I'll show you how two goes into one."

Jake and Katrina were listening intently in the truck and burst into laughter.

"She done good Katrina."

"Yes she did. And hopefully she won't hold it against me for too long! Now it's our turn, I guess."

"Is Cathy ready?"

"A little too ready. I'm afraid of the scene she's going to cause."

34   *Chaos*

Katrina left the truck ahead of Jake, careful to make sure no one saw them together. She was going in to find Marlene and congratulate her on her performance. She wondered if Marlene had taken acting classes from Cathy. Katrina passed Granderson in the entrance area and smiled at the statue like figure.

Jake waited about two minutes after Katrina then headed toward the back entrance. He didn't want Ben to spot him as he entered. The plan would become messed up if Jake went in the front door and Ben pulled him into his office for their talk. It was only a minute or so before his scheduled meeting with Ben and Tammy in the Ramirez visitation room. Jake came through the back door and stomped a small amount of fresh snow off of his Kodiak's, looking up just in time to avoid Lawrence flattening him.

"Excuse me," said Jake facetiously to Lawrence as he rushed by. Lawrence was, no doubt, going out to get the bulk of Marlene's order from his car. Jake assumed that Lawrence was dumb enough to keep the stolen goods in his car, but still wanted to catch him in the act of stealing one or pawning them to solidify his case.

The room for the Ramirez funeral was ahead on the left. Jake entered to find Tammy picking at one of the floral arrangements to make it look larger than it really was. To his surprise, there were already a few grievers in the room. This was a detour for his plan, as he wanted to confront the two of them together. It didn't seem appropriate to do it in front of these mourners.

"What can I do for you officer?" Tammy asked. She then noticed Ben coming in the room over Jake's shoulder. "Ben, what's up?" she asked him.

"Nothing. I'm just here to meet with the officer here."

"Me too . . . What's this all about? Why do you need to talk to both of us?"

"I wanted to talk to you at the same time about a couple of things."

"Such as . . . ?" Tammy inquired, crossing her arms in a noticeably defensive stance. Ben looked at her oddly, wondering why she would act in such a way.

"Well, I think we're close to making a bust on the jewelry thefts."

"Great!" said Ben. "Anything I, I mean we, can do to help?"

"No, it's under control, but thanks. I also wanted to talk to you both about the caskets."

"What about the caskets?" Tammy stood nervously shuffling her weight from one leg to the other. Ben did the same, almost in unison like a miniature chorus line. Jake smiled at the sight, but also recognized that they both looked guilty, or at least on edge.

"It seems that someone here has been scamming people . . . " Jake paused in mid-sentence upon noticing the entry of Lawrence into the room. Tammy and Ben noticed the hesitation and looked to see what Jake was looking at. Jake quickly returned his focus to the two of them.

"What do mean scamming people?" asked Tammy, not waiting for him to finish his hanging sentence.

"I mean that people have paid for expensive caskets and not gotten them."

"That's impossible," exclaimed Tammy. "I confirm every casket matches the invoice before the service even occurs."

"Yes, what are you implying?" asked Ben. "Do you think we're taking bodies out in the coach and putting them in another casket or something?"

"Or maybe I go out to the cemetery, dig them up, take the body out, put it in a casket made of plywood, and rebury them." Tammy's voice began to rise, and she stood with both hands on her hips, legs slightly apart in a stance that said 'you wanna go?'

"It does sound rather ridiculous what you're proposing officer," Ben stated in support.

The room slowly filled with mourners throughout their conversation. Jake caught the entrance of Katrina and Marlene at different times during the discussion. He didn't notice Cathy come in to the room, but he had to trust 'Ramona' was ready for Katrina's signal.

Jake specifically had kept an eye on Lawrence milling about. A family member was going up to the casket with each mourner, not providing Lawrence the opportunity to get close enough to steal Mr. Ramirez's Movado watch. Katrina had also noticed this and was growing impatient. She told herself to have patience, but looked at her watch and realized the service was to start in ten minutes. She decided to give him five more minutes to make a move or she would get Ramona involved.

"It does sound ridiculous but I'm sure one of you is in on it. I'm just not sure both of you aren't working together," Jake shot back. "I know how it's done, and even who the accomplices are."

"Perhaps you'd be kind enough to let us in on the magic trick," Ben replied.

Before Jake could answer, Katrina had apparently given 'Ramona' the signal.

In a loud and tipsy sounding voice came an announcement.

"Where is Mrs. Ramirez? Where is Mrs. Friggin' Ramirez? I want to meet the bitch that kept me and Hector apart?"

"I'm right here," a short, stocky woman responded back, emerging from a small gathering. The lady looked at her and continued "You must be that sleaze bag Ramona that tricked my husband into sleeping with her!" and she spit at Ramona's shoes.

The planned disturbance was working as hoped. During the exchange, Lawrence had made his way over to the end of the casket. Jake hadn't seen Lawrence make his move yet but it was only a matter of time.

'Ramona' looked down at her shoes in disgust and anger. Cathy had slipped right into character and was now pissed off. She took a quick step forward and with both hands pushed Mrs. Ramirez to the floor. The room full of mourners looked on, stunned. Tammy moved to break up the two but didn't get there soon enough. Mrs. Ramirez had landed near a small pedestal with a small flower arrangement on it. She stood up and grabbed the arrangement from it resting place and threw it. Cathy/Ramona reacted quickly and was able to lean to the side just enough to avert it as the flower missile went hurtling by. Unfortunately, Tammy didn't see the oncoming projectile vase until Cathy had leaned out of the way. The vase glanced off the side of Tammy's head and knocked her down, and out.

The redirection caused by careening off Tammy's skull sent the vase smashing into the assembled chairs. The commotion was perfect for Lawrence to make his move. He bent slightly over the casket, slid up the sleeve of Mr. Ramirez, and with a quick flip, removed the watch. Before Lawrence could even pocket his new prize and slip on a fake substitute, he felt a hand on his shoulder. It was Jake's.

"Freeze, Lawrence! Give me the watch." Jake had learned that criminals rarely do freeze when you ask them. They usually panic.

Of course, Lawrence didn't freeze or hand over the watch. He palmed the watch in an attempt to hide the evidence, before realizing he was busted and better run. He panicked. He abruptly swung back his elbow into Jake's ribs. Jake winced and bent over briefly before the two of them started wrestling. They turned around a couple of times in each other's grip. The two of them banged firmly into the casket, causing the lid to shut hard. One of them must have stepped on the foot break on the bier holding the casket and it spun slightly away from the wall. Jake got a good hold on Lawrence's collar and held on as he drilled him violently into the now mobile casket. The casket's momentum caused it to slam into the wall, smashing a few flower baskets and vases with it. The casket spray slid off and landed upside down on the floor. As the rolling casket hit the wall, the facing of the casket popped off and fell loudly to the floor below.

Meanwhile, Cathy had gone back after Mrs. Ramirez and the two of them were locked in combat rolling on the floor, pulling hair and screaming obscenities at each other. They knocked over some of the folding chairs set out for the service. Mourners scurried for a safe spot to stand.

After the last push into the casket, Lawrence was winded and bent over at the side of the casket. He too decided a flower arrangement would make a good weapon and grabbed a particularly heavy looking vase and pushed it toward Jake. Having anticipated this action, and standing only a few feet away, Jake was able to deflect it right back toward Lawrence. The heavy vase landed squarely on Lawrence's foot, causing him to once again double over. In desperation, Lawrence tried evading Jake by going around the speaker's podium. Limping and keeping an eye on Jake, Lawrence didn't notice the trajectory of the rolling ladies. They bowled him over sending him flying like a corner pin. Jake walked over and cuffed the stunned Lawrence on the spot.

A young lady ran over to Cathy and Mrs. Ramirez, waving her arms frantically and screaming at them to stop. It was Mrs. Ramirez's daughter Wanda. Both combatants looked up, still grasping onto one another.

"This isn't even Ramona, Mama. I hired her to pretend to be Ramona." Wanda turned to Cathy. "You were good, really good."

"But why?" asked the mother, letting go of Cathy and pushing her away. She stood up, adjusting her dress and fluffing her hair as she did.

"Because you were miserable to papa for the last ten years of his life. He stayed by you because of me, but he loved Ramona. He also knew that you'd take him for every penny, even though you hadn't shown him any love in years. I didn't want him buried without people knowing. He wouldn't let the real Ramona come for fear that you'd attack her." Wanda looked around at the mess created in the room. "I guess you proved him right."

Tammy was just starting to sit up from getting K-O'd by the vase. Aside from the early signs of a nasty bruise, she thought she was okay. When she saw bodies flying everywhere, Tammy rubbed her eyes first, then the bump on her melon. This must be a hallucination. Her eyes scanned the chaos for Ben, however, focusing was still a problem. She thought she saw him heading toward the door. Was she really seeing it or just dreaming? Tammy had presided over many funerals in the short time that she was employed at Shady Rest and had experienced many unusual things. She decided that this couldn't be really happening and lay back down on the floor and closed her eyes.

Tammy was correct about Ben heading toward the back door during the commotion. He knew the jig was up on the casket scheme, one having fallen apart right in front of the entire group assembled. Ben wanted to get to his office to shred the invoices for the caskets, not really thinking that it would matter, but not knowing what else to do besides catching a flight to some obscure country. He looked over his shoulder just before reaching the doorway to see if anyone had detected him slipping out. As he turned back to the exit, he stepped right into two uniformed officers whom had taken position to block the way out. He looked back at the other door just as two more officers blocked that exit.

"Can I have your attention, please?!" Jake walked toward the podium, a little ragged looking from his skirmish with Lawrence. He tucked in his shirt as he walked back from talking to one of the uniformed officers.

"Thank you, officers, for containing the room." Jake looked at them as he acknowledged the uniforms at the front and back doors. "I apologize to the Ramirez family for the disturbance at the front. I hope it didn't interrupt your own melee." Jake looked around at the mess at the front. Broken vases, flowers strewn all over the place, chairs toppled, and a few people looking worse for wear. Lawrence still lay on his belly, cuffed behind his back. "Lawrence – the officers here have just executed an authorized search of your car and confiscated . . . what was it Sam . . . how many watches?"

"Sixty-three, Jake" was the response from the uniformed officer. "Plus, many jewelry items." The office was holding a box with the contents of the raid. He reached in and held up a spectacular looking gold and diamond necklace.

Katrina was excited inside and almost let out a scream of joy. They had recovered Mrs. Wilmont's jewelry!

"Sixty-three stolen watches and numerous other jewelry items. Plus, you were caught in the act of trying to steal another one."

"I was set up . . . I'll get off" Lawrence shouted back, looking partly like a fish out of water as he wriggled on the floor.

"You were set up by your own stupidity," Jake replied to a chorus of laughter.

"And Ben . . . we know you're behind the casket scam. We talked to Elliott down at Stan's Custom Craft Woodworking. He told us how you gave him the plans and that you told him it was for display purposes only. Elliott had actually called the police the other day after you placed the second order. He knew something wasn't right. I think the term he was looking for was fraud. I just wasn't sure until today if Tammy was involved, but she's not."

The officers at the door by Ben grabbed him and placed him in cuffs. The officers at the other door picked up Lawrence off the floor.

"Watch the police brutality you thugs." Lawrence wrestled himself away from the grasp of the officers for a second as he stood up. The sudden motion caused him to stagger and with no free arms to balance with, he went piling into the chairs before hitting the floor.

"Take him away guys before he hurts himself some more."

At this point, much like the fish that had been flapping around at the bottom of the boat trying to get back into the water, Lawrence finally realized the futility and gave up. He went peacefully with his escorts. Jake followed behind.

"Jake . . . wait up" Katrina shouted after him.

Jake stopped and turned toward Katrina. A stern look was on his face that she had never seen before. She thought he'd be happy.

"What's wrong?"

Jake paused for a few seconds. He put his hands in the back pockets of his jeans. His hands went up to cover his face as he looked to control his emotions. A few more seconds of silence passed.

"Look. I've worked very hard on this case. We've worked very hard on this case. You were supposed to wait for my signal before you signaled Cathy."

"I'm sorry. I guess I got excited."

"Well sorry doesn't cut it sometimes. You put the entire investigation and everyone in that room at risk. I lost control of the situation. Hopefully Lawrence isn't right and I can get this to stick."

"I'm sorry . . . "

"I've got to go. This would have been a pile of paperwork without this debacle. Now I'll probably be doing paperwork until summer."

Jake's upset look morphed into a disappointed look before he turned and walked away.

Only moments before, Katrina was on an adrenalin high from the thrill of the chaotic conclusion of their investigation. She wanted to hold Jake tightly and thank him for solving Duncan's case. Now, after Jake's tongue lashing, she was bummed. Katrina solemnly stood there, head bowed, fearful she had blown any hope of having something more than a working relationship with Jake. Having two fights in a few days likely killed any chances.

35 *The End*

Katrina stared out the window of the salon - another snowy winter day in Toronto.

"I can see why you can't stand this weather Kevin. I'm just glad we live in the city, and not somewhere too remote. I can only imagine what cabin fever feels like." She was happy to have solved the jewelry case and the casket scam. Katrina was somewhat relieved that no mention of Stewart and the charity thing had even come up. She worried about her friend Cathy becoming implicated in it, or that Stewart would somehow stick Cathy with the entire rap.

In spite of her successes, Katrina was depressed. It was a matter of a couple of days before she would lose her business. She would be broke and unemployed. She no longer had a roommate to split the rent on her apartment. She no longer had a boyfriend to comfort her. And Jake's reaction as he left the crime scene left little doubt in her mind that romance with him was a dead end. Life was looking pretty shitty.

"Every cloud's got a silver lining, deary," Kevin put his arm around her, trying to cheer her up. Seems a good friend reminded me of that once not too long ago while I was standing at this very window."

"Yeah, but that was just about losing tip money. This is serious. We could all be without jobs."

"You got $5,000 for recovering that lady's jewels, didn't you?"

"Yes, but it's not enough."

"But it is enough." Kevin smiled, but before he could finish he was interrupted.

In front of the window, three figures emerged from the onslaught of snow. The winter wind whipped through the door as it was opened, causing the year old magazines to flap with the incoming gust. It was Stewart, Cathy, and Jake.

"Look, its Larry, Moe, and Shirley," Kevin quipped.

"How indignant, being compared to those bumbling morons," Stewart said, raising his nose in a stuck-up British ruling class way.

"What are you three doing here? And what are you doing together?" She was getting goose bumps from the excitement of seeing Jake again but was containing her enthusiasm. It was tempered slightly by her concern about Cathy getting busted.

"Cathy was down at the station giving a statement and Mr. Windle accompanied her. They obliged me with a ride here."

"Why?" Katrina asked back, now convinced they were getting busted for the charity scheme.

"I'm here about your commendation. The police chief is giving you one for assisting with solving the crimes. And you too,

Marlene." Jake turned to see Katrina's employee grinning from ear to ear. "It was a little extra paperwork, but what does a few more pages matter after all that I had to do anyway." Katrina was happy to see Jake's customary dimpled smile return to his face. She didn't want her last impression of him to be the Jake that scolded her in Shady Rest.

"And what else . . . " Cathy prodded Jake.

"Well . . . " Jake stammered.

"Just spit it out. You couldn't shut up about her the whole ride here. Katrina this and Katrina that. Oh, have you looked in her eyes . . . and so on."

"Really?" Katrina looked at Jake. He reached for her hands. They stared into each other eyes.

"I hope you don't get tired of hearing me say that I'm sorry," Jake reflected on Katrina's apologies at the funeral home. "Again, I'm used to dealing with police detectives. They would know better than to deviate from plan unless an emergency arose. I shouldn't have held you to the same standard as them. "I'm sorr . . . "

Before he could get the last syllable out, Katrina put a finger up against his lips to stop him from finishing. She then moved closer and they locked in a passionate kiss.

"Some girls don't take long to get over another guy . . . " Kevin mused.

Marlene sniped at him. "Just let them have their moment, will you?"

"I was just trying to tell her that her salon is saved, that's all."

In spite of her focus on kissing Jake, Katrina heard this and turned to Kevin.

"What do you mean? I only have half."

"Ron was so impressed by your desperation to save the salon that he agreed to lend you the other $5,000. No payments. No interest for six months to qualified stylists."

"That's wonderful, Kevin!" Katrina took a step over to Kevin and kissed him on the cheek. She didn't let go of Jake's hand though.

Before anyone could say anything else, the door opened again. It was Duncan's lawyer, who had dated Marlene once – if you consider going to a funeral and out for coffee at Starbucks a date. Katrina assumed he was here to see Marlene again and immediately went back to kissing Jake.

The lawyer cleared his throat before saying, "Excuse me, Miss Katrina." He was trying to get her attention without having to pry lips apart.

"Oh, sorry. I thought you were here for Marlene."

"Perhaps another time . . . " and he smiled in Marlene's direction. "For now, I have something to read to you."

"Oh for chrissakes . . . what did I do now?"

Giving her a disappointed look he replied. "Lawyers don't always bring bad news you know." He pulled out a small document of about five stapled pages from his bag. He began to read "Let's see. There is a bunch of the usual legal rhetoric . . . da, da, da . . . Here we are. To the one person outside of my family who never judged me or my peculiar ways. Who never gave me a dirty look for the way I dressed, Katrina, I leave the sum of $100,000 and my Gucci watch."

He put the paper down and looked at Katrina who stood there, mouth agape. Her nails were digging deeply into Jake's arms, and he winced in pain. She started to cry.

"Tell Ron thanks, Kevin, but it doesn't look like I'll need that loan!" and she wiped her eyes, which was fortunate for Jake as her nails stopped digging into him. Then she started to laugh uncontrollable.

"Emotional thing, isn't she?" Stewart stated. "Crying one second and laughing the next! Good luck to you with that one" as he looked at Jake.

"What's so funny Kat?" Cathy asked her, putting her hand on Katrina's shoulder, after a quick jab to Stewart's ribs for his remark.

"He left me his stolen watch. It was one of the few items we never recovered! Don't you see . . . if it wasn't for the watch, we wouldn't have had this whole adventure and I would have never met Jake."

Looking for more from Katrina?

Check out the FIRST book in the series,

Life of the Party

written by Maureen P. Moore

(over)

Life of the Party

'Outgoing? Gorgeous? Enjoy P/T evening work? Good fun! Good pay! THIS IS PERFECTLY LEGAL!' The ad in the Toronto paper sounds just about perfect for Katrina. Except for the 'outgoing' part. Desperate to escape a creepy roommate and a scary landlord, she must find some way to supplement her meager café salary to flee to a new apartment.

Eye-popping beautiful but woefully shy, when Katrina is hired as a professional guest (aka PEST) for a company called Life of the Party, her nerves get the best of her. Before she can make a total fool of herself and lose her new job, she's saved by a dashing and mysterious stranger who vanishes into the night.

With the help of her newfound friend and fellow PEST Cathy, Katrina tries desperately to find her mystery man. Her search, and her life, gets disrupted by the nefarious affairs of her roommates, landlord, and new boss. Along the way, Katrina learns that she may be shy - but she's certainly no wallflower.

www.northernamusements.com